PINKIES stories

SHANE HINTON

PAPERBACK bp ORIGINALS

3 1969 02317 0250

Book design by Tina Craig
Cover art by John Hurst
Published by Burrow Press

ISBN: 978-1-941681-92-3
E-ISBN: 978-1-941681-93-0
LCCN: 2014958771

Distributed by Itasca Books.
orders@itascabooks.com

Burrow Press
PO Box 533709
Orlando, FL 32853

PRINT: burrowpress.com
WEB: burrowpressreview.com
FLESH: functionallyliterate.org

The stories in this collection were previously published in slightly different form. "All the Shane Hintons" in *The Butter*. "Nobody Loves Mr. Iglesias" in *Word Riot*. "Excision" in *Atticus Review*. "Never Trust the Weatherman" in *Dead Mule School of Southern Literature*. "Intersection" in *Fiction Advocate*. "Fumes" in *storySouth*. "Miguelito" in *The Nervous Breakdown*.

PRAISE FOR
PINKIES

"If Kafka got it on with Flannery O' Connor, *Pinkies* would be their love child."
–Lidia Yuknavitch, author of *The Small Backs of Children*

"Shane Hinton's *Pinkies* is weird, and it is wonderful. This debut collection–in which the everyday is always extraordinary–reminds me of fiction by Joy Williams and Mary Robison, and also of movies by Charlie Kaufman. If that sounds like ridiculously high praise, then good: *Pinkies* deserves it."
–Brock Clarke, author of *The Happiest People in the World*

"Shane Hinton's writing is terrifically smart and coolly cerebral, and full of quietly reserved, understated power. He treats the despair of the essential human condition with strength and dignity. A remarkable new young American writer, whose talent is likely to become progressively more vital and profound in the years to come."
–Mikhail Iossel, author of *Every Hunter Wants to Know*

"The stories in Shane Hinton's *Pinkies* wriggle with volatility. Bracingly unpredictable, they'll slip out of your hands if you're not careful. Here is all the absurdity and latent dread of life, but funnier, stranger, more potent."
–Kevin Moffett, author of *The Silent History*

"Shane Hinton's fiction is the visceral kind that you feel with your whole body, and it makes me want to cry through my laughing and cringing. I don't know a better compliment to give a writer."
–Jeff Parker, author of *Where Bears Roam The Streets*

For Jess, Further, Vera, and Iris, who always let me have time to do this stupid thing I can't stop doing.

PINKIES

PINKIES

I looked at grainy black and white pictures of Jess' insides on the ultrasound machine. The nurse held the device with her right hand and coughed into her left. "Is everything okay?" Jess asked. On the screen, shapes moved and merged into one another. It looked like she was filled up with clouds.

"You've got lots of people in there," the nurse said, wiping her nose with the back of her hand.

"How many?" I asked.

"Too early to tell," the nurse said. "I hope you have room for all these babies."

We didn't have room. When we got home, we stood in the hallway, looking at the doors to our two bedrooms.

"I'm going to be so big," Jess said.

"I can build bunk beds," I said.

"We need to start saving for college."

We spent the evening making spreadsheets on our laptops. The budget didn't look good. Jess thought we were being irresponsible with our debt.

The next day we went to the library and picked out stacks of novels and history books and encyclopedias, looking for names. We made a list of the names of our favorite protagonists and generals and scientists and cartographers. We reread novels that we loved when we were eighteen, but we couldn't remember why.

We looked for names in our family trees, but weren't sure if the dead people had been slave owners or wife beaters. I told Jess that it didn't matter, that our babies probably wouldn't be either. "These things are important," she said, and we left it at that.

•

At our next doctor's visit, I carried the list of names in my shirt pocket. It had been folded over and over and the paper was growing thin. While we sat in the waiting room, I kept touching it to make sure it was still there.

The doctor was an older man with curly gray hair and glasses. "How's mama feeling?" he asked, poking Jess' belly. "Must be crowded in there."

"Some days I just can't get out of bed," she said.

"I'm not sure she has enough room for food," I said. "How is she supposed to eat?"

"Is it okay to name the babies after someone who was maybe a slave owner or a wife beater?" Jess asked.

The doctor held up his hands. "I know you have a lot of questions. Having children is confusing. People are going to be pressing in on you from every side. I know all about it. My wife has had thirteen." He listened to Jess' belly with his stethoscope.

"Everything turned out okay?" I asked.

"We lost some of them," he said. "It's one of those things you don't think you'll ever get over, but you do. Life goes on."

"What happened?" Jess asked.

"Oh, all things beyond our control." He tapped on Jess' knee and her leg shot up. "Playground accidents, python attacks. You can't expect everything to be okay. That's just not realistic."

"Python attacks?" I asked.

"Yes, they're very invasive," the doctor said, writing something on his notepad. "Changing the ecosystem. Particularly rough on the feeble and the elderly. And small children, of course."

Out the window, through a metal grate, I could see an old woman in a wheelchair next to a rose bush. A hospital gown was loose around her thighs. Something moved inside the rose bushes, but when I blinked it was gone. The doctor smiled. Jess stood up and stretched her back.

"Do you have any snake traps?" the doctor asked. "You might want to buy one or two, just in case."

·

I ordered a dozen snake traps that night and chose the expedited shipping option. The website said they were guaranteed cruelty-free. The pictures showed different kinds of snakes stuck in boxes with clear glass sides: cottonmouths, rattlesnakes, black racers. The snakes were attracted to the bait and, once inside, they couldn't find the hole again to get back out. "What are we supposed to do with them once they're in the traps?" I asked Jess.

She shrugged.

"I don't think we can just release them back into the wild," I said.

After work the next day, I stopped at the pet store on the way home. They had rows of pythons in glass cages. A teenage girl with a nose ring sat behind the counter reading a book.

"What do they eat?" I asked, gesturing to the pythons.

The girl set down her book. "Pinkies," she said.

"Pinkies?"

"Newborn mice." She led me to an aquarium with wood shavings lining the bottom. At first I couldn't see anything. I leaned in until my nose almost touched the glass. A pile of hairless baby mice was half-buried in the wood shavings. Their wrinkled skin blended together and I couldn't tell one from the next. Their eyes bulged out behind thin, almost transparent eyelids. They looked like tiny dogs, sniffing the air, stretching their paws into each other's sides and backs.

"How many do I need?" I asked.

"You got a new pet?"

"My wife is pregnant," I said. "These are for traps."

The girl nodded slowly. "I see. How many points of entry do you have? Doors and windows?"

I counted in my head. "Three doors and eight windows."

"All right. A couple dozen should do you." She reached into the aquarium, plucking out the pinkies and dropping them into a clear plastic bag. When she was done, she tied a knot in the top of the bag and handed it to me. It was full of air, like a beach ball, and the wriggling mass of pinkies at the bottom felt warm against my hand.

•

I put the snake traps next to every door and window and baited them each with two of the tiny mice. Spring was over, and as the pinkies panted, their breath fogged up the clear plastic walls of the traps.

The heat made the pythons more active. Almost every afternoon there was a new report of an attack in our area. Local preschools went on lockdown after a kid disappeared during recess. One of the news channels started referring to summer as "python season."

A couple days after I placed the traps, I came home from work to find Jess sunbathing in the empty lot next to our house. The grass was overgrown and there were three dead trees fallen in the weeds. Perfect hiding places, I thought.

"What are you doing?" I said. "It's python season. They're probably out there right now, thinking how easily the little babies will slide down their throats. You know they unhinge their jaws to eat."

"That's sensationalism," Jess said. "There's no more pythons than there ever have been. You just hear about them now, with all the news coverage. They have to fill air time."

A Fish and Wildlife Commission helicopter circled overhead. "Look," I said, pointing up. "Why do you think they're here?"

"Well, if there is a python, I'm sure they'll find it."

"Not from the air," I said. "They blend in so well with their surroundings."

Jess put her hand on her belly. Her skin was shiny with tanning oil and sweat. "You think a python could swallow me like this? I'm huge." She lifted a plastic water bottle to her mouth and drank half of it without stopping.

"The news says that python attacks are up five hundred percent this year," I said.

Jess shrugged and picked up her paperback, and we left it at that.

•

Jess' belly grew rounder and the babies moved inside, their arms and legs making shapes under her skin. We spent a lot of time in bed, watching TV and reading books. I kept the list of names close at hand, on the bedside table, or stuck between the pages of a novel to mark my place.

One night, we selected a nature program. The British host was attractive and muscular, with a light pink scar on his left cheek. "What's his name?" Jess asked.

"Jack Cougar," I said, "but I think it's a stage name."

"Put it on the list," she said.

In the program, Jack Cougar followed a large python around a neighborhood bordering the Everglades, using night vision to show its hunting patterns. "The pythons here in South Florida are descended from pets," whispered Jack Cougar. "They're not afraid of humans. They see us as a food source. People got too comfortable with nature and brought these apex predators into their homes. When the snakes grew too big, the owners released them out into the wild. Now the pythons are coming back." Jack Cougar crept along a suburban street, poking his head over a row of hedges to get a view of a large python. The snake stopped underneath a window and raised its head up to the glass. The camera zoomed in on a small dog inside the window. "She's hungry," Jack Cougar whispered, "and now she knows there's food in the house. She won't forget. The python is a highly intelligent hunter."

•

Glenda, our elderly next-door neighbor, stopped us two days later as we were leaving to visit the doctor. She was feeding goldfish in the small concrete pond in her yard.

"Oh, my. You're so big," she said to Jess. The goldfish struck at the pieces of fish food floating on the surface of the pond. "Boys or girls?"

"Some of both," Jess said. She put her hand on her stomach.

"That's great," Glenda said. "We're all looking forward to having some little girls running around the neighborhood."

Our neighbor across the street, Bob, stopped mowing his lawn and came over to see us. "Going to have some new babies around here, huh?" he said, wiping the sweat off his forehead. "Glenda says you've got a whole clan in there." He pointed at Jess' stomach. "Oh, hey, are those snake traps? I've been thinking of getting some, too. I found a pygmy rattlesnake in my garage the other day. The dog almost got to it before I could."

"Yeah," I said. "I bought them online. They're supposed to be cruelty-free. The doctor said we should have some to keep away the pythons."

Bob laughed. "Go putting out those little mice and they'll be coming around every few days for a snack before dinner."

"That reminds me," Glenda said. "Shane, what are we going to do about all of these cats?" A family of feral cats had moved into the neighborhood and every month or two they produced another litter. The cats fought during the night and woke us up, yowling outside our bedroom window, but I was happy that they kept the rats out of our garbage and suppressed the squirrel population. Glenda put out food for the cats every night. "I called Animal Control, but they said I have to trap them myself," she said. "I don't think I can do that."

"You could stop feeding them," I said.

"I don't think I can do that, either," Glenda said.

•

Nothing took the bait in the snake traps. The pinkies died and started to stink. I opened up the traps and dumped the tiny mice into the garbage can, feeling like a failure.

At our next appointment, the doctor said the babies were growing at the expected rate. "I haven't caught anything in the snake traps," I said. "The pinkies all died. Should we be worried?"

"Well, pythons do need live bait," the doctor said. He flipped through pages on his clipboard, then took out a measuring string and wrapped it around Jess' belly. "Yes, I'd like to see something in those traps. How many mice did you use?"

"Two in each trap," I said.

"Okay. Let's try three. Make an appointment for next week at the front desk." He smiled. "We'll get this figured out."

When we got home, the neighbors were all standing in the street the way they do when the power goes out. We stopped the car in front of our driveway and asked Bob what was going on.

"Python sighting," Bob said. "Better get mama inside." He held a golf club in his right hand. "We're keeping an eye on the neighborhood."

Glenda held a large kitchen knife. "You two go on," she said. "We're watching out here."

·

I went back to the pet store and the same girl was reading behind the cash register. "I need more pinkies," I said.

"You've been watching the news," she said.

"I think so. Why?"

"You look nervous. They're just trying to keep you worked up about pythons so they can sell more advertising."

"The doctor told us to set traps."

The girl shrugged. "A lot of people say a lot of things." She dug behind the counter and handed me a pamphlet. It was titled *Living with Invasive Species: A Guide to Peaceful Coexistence.* "Check it out," she said. "How many pinkies do you want?"

·

I baited the traps, pinching the newborn mice at the scruff of the neck and placing them gently into the plastic boxes. I looked up guides for raising mice on the internet. That night, I went back outside and fed the pinkies baby formula with an eye dropper, one by one. They nuzzled the glass tube and sucked enthusiastically.

Later, as we lay in bed, Jess said, "I wonder what the babies will be like."

"I think they'll be happy for the most part, but sometimes they'll have bad days," I said. "That's just unavoidable."

"I think they'll understand the importance of family, but won't be burdened by the obligations of it. We'll try not to guilt them."

"Definitely," I said. "When I get old, I'll tell them, 'Just let me die in this old house by myself.'"

"They won't believe you, but maybe it will make them feel better."

"The girl at the pet shop gave me a pamphlet," I said. "It says we should try to live with the pythons."

"We were here first," Jess said.

We left it at that.

I had trouble sleeping that night. Every noise sounded like a python: the ice maker, the washing machine, the neighbors smoking cigarettes. Jess rolled from side to side in bed. The babies buried their feet into her ribs, she said. She couldn't breathe.

•

The next morning, before work, I noticed the window at the back of Glenda's house was shattered. The bent screen was on the ground, surrounded by broken glass. I was afraid that it might be a burglar, so I called Glenda's name from the edge of the yard. No one answered. I walked around the house, checking the other windows, and found long, fat snake tracks in the dirt beneath the oak tree.

I called 911 and the neighborhood filled with emergency vehicles. News vans parked in Glenda's driveway and extended satellite dishes on long poles into the sky. Bob and I stood in the street watching reporters speak into microphones and hold their hands to their ears so they could hear better through their earpieces.

"I told you not to put out those little mice," Bob said.

"Pinkies," I said. "And nothing ate them. The traps are still baited."

"I still don't think it's a good idea," he said.

"Doctor's orders," I said.

"Tell that to Glenda's kids," Bob said.

The news reporters said the police found evidence of forced entry, but no signs of a struggle. It looked like she had been taken from her bedroom. They couldn't find a body. She had just disappeared.

•

The doctor told Jess that she was getting too big too quickly and that the babies might be born early and have to be put in machines that would move their tiny lungs for them. We didn't speak on the way home.

Jess went inside to rest and I fed the pinkies baby formula from the eyedropper. It had already been a week, and they were starting to grow hair and move around inside the traps. I asked Jess if we should name them, but she thought it was a bad idea.

"They're not going to live long enough," she said.

While I fed them, I pulled the list of baby names out of my shirt pocket and read the ones that we had scratched out. They seemed appropriate for the baby mice. I decided which one would get which name and didn't tell Jess about it when I came in for dinner.

In bed, we read together from the pamphlet. It made some good points. The snakes were not going anywhere, it said. The government had been paying people to bring in dead pythons by the pound in South Florida, and there were more down there than ever. Their birth rate was too high, and their camouflage was too well-suited to the tropical environment. It said the important thing to understand about living with pythons was that they were ambushers. They were patient, and you had to be aware of places that would make good hiding spots.

Jess had already fallen asleep with her head on my chest, and I didn't want to wake her up, so I looked around the room without moving my head. There were a lot of places for pythons to hide in our bedroom. I didn't even want to think about the living room and kitchen.

•

The neighborhood held a vigil for Glenda. Her kids and grandkids gathered in her driveway, lighting candles and holding hands and praying. The pastor of her church gave a brief speech in front of her garage door. "I've known Glenda for fifty-three years. I performed her marriage to her late husband, Richard. I presented the eulogy at Richard's funeral. Let's bow our heads and ask that Glenda might be found, alive and well." Glenda's grandchildren clung to their parents' legs. Feral cats circled the crowd, running between hedges and oak trees, poking their heads out of the flower beds.

Only one news crew showed up, and they shot footage of the crowd praying and singing "Amazing Grace." On the evening news they showed the shots of the mourners, standing in the long driveway, their faces illuminated from below by the candles on the ground. Jess and I recorded it to our DVR. It was sad, but it felt strange to see ourselves on TV.

I paused the show when Jess and I were in the frame. "Do you think we look sad enough?" I said. "I guess I could have looked at the ground more."

"Maybe we should name one of the babies Glenda," Jess said. I touched the list of names in my shirt pocket. I had used most of them up on the baby mice.

"I'll put it on the list," I said.

"Do it now," Jess said. "I don't want you to forget."

I took the list out of my pocket and held it in the palm of my hand as I wrote. I felt like I needed to hide it from Jess, that somehow seeing the scribbled names would tell her that the little pink mice outside our doors and windows were using up our babies' names, that she would want to throw the list away and start all over with new names from new books that we hadn't even read yet. There wasn't enough time. The babies were growing too fast. They could come any minute.

•

"Your blood pressure is way too high," the doctor said. "And you've got protein in your urine."

"What does that mean?" Jess asked.

"The babies are coming soon," the doctor said. "They're telling us it's not as safe in there anymore. They think they're going to do better out here." He chuckled. "We've got the breathing machines all ready for them. It seems relaxing, not having to breathe on your own. And the rhythmic noises of the machines are very comforting."

"I haven't caught anything in the traps yet," I said.

The doctor crossed his arms over his white coat. "Nothing?" he asked. "Rat snake? Indigo?"

"Nothing," I said. I looked down at the floor.

"How are you keeping the mice alive?" the doctor asked.

"Baby formula," I said. "I read about it on the internet."

"That sounds right." The doctor made a note on his clipboard. "This is only going to become more important after the babies are born. You need to work on your technique."

"I've never been good at trapping," I said. "When I was a kid, I tried to build a raccoon trap, but the raccoons just ate the meat and left the poison sitting on the ground."

"Poisoning isn't the same as trapping," the doctor said.

"I guess not," I said.

"It's an important distinction," he said.

•

Glenda had been missing for five days when I heard shouts coming from the street. I told Jess to go back inside. Neighbors were running toward Bob's house. I followed them around the side and into his back yard. Several other neighbors were already there, gathered in a circle. Bob was in the center, his golf club raised high. It made a wet sound when it hit.

I pushed into the circle of people. In the center a python was wrapped around Bob's dog, a cocker spaniel named Yankee Doodle. The neighbors moved in and hit the snake with baseball bats and two-by-fours until it went limp, then they backed off a few feet, sweating and panting. Yankee Doodle wiggled out from the python's hold and ran to Bob, whimpering.

When the police arrived, they hung the snake by its tail from the branch of an oak tree in Bob's yard. Its belly was fat, like an overinflated tire. When they cut it open, Glenda's body spilled out onto the ground. The snake had partially digested her. She was naked, and there were holes in her skin where muscle and bone showed through. Paramedics put her on a stretcher and covered her with a white sheet. Stomach acid soaked through the sheet and stuck the fabric to the curves of her body.

News reporters wanted to interview everyone. It was a happy ending, they said. Bob brought out a twelve pack and a grill and started cooking hamburgers. People took pictures next to the snake, giving thumbs-up to the camera.

I left the party and emptied the pinkies from the snake traps, putting them in a yogurt container I'd pulled out of the trash. They were weak, but the movement woke them up and they squeaked and wiggled around with their eyes still closed.

Jess waited for me in the doorway. "They caught it?" she asked.

I nodded. "Guess we don't need these guys," I said.

"You're not bringing them in here," she said.

I set the yogurt container down on the front stoop and followed her inside. As I shut the door, I saw one of the feral cats that Glenda used to feed crawling across the yard, its eyes on the yogurt container, looking ready to pounce.

PETS

PETS

All the animals I had between the age of five and twelve died grisly deaths.

We found the goat eating glass off the floor of the barn. I pulled the animal to its pen and Dad nailed the fence back in place. The goat lay down in the grass, bleating in pain. He was dead before the sun went down.

Our chickens were eaten by a fox. I found the coop covered in blood when I went to feed them before school. My favorite one had an extra toe. The fox had left her foot a few feet from the coop.

My python wiggled out of his cage so often I had to stack dictionaries on the lid to keep it closed. He eventually knocked the lid off despite the extra weight. We found him in the attic when his decaying body stank up the house.

Our cat got an infection in its brain the same day I got suspended from school for fighting. She fell out of the oak tree in the front yard and broke her back. We put her in a cardboard box lined with paper towels, where she pissed herself until the vet put her down.

An alligator ate one of our dogs in a pond on the farm. For a while afterward I carried a rifle to the pond every day and shot at bubbles in the water.

Another dog followed the tractor for half a mile drinking weed killer before anyone noticed. Dad held her head as she died next to the ditch.

We dug rows and rows of graves out in the pasture, marked by small wooden crosses with each animal's name and date of death. The crosses would last a month or two and then get blown down in a thunderstorm or trampled by the cows as they grazed. The earth sank in, leaving a series of shallow depressions.

Even without the crosses, I could tell which animal was buried in which hole by the size of the grave. I walked through the rows after school, trying to remember each of them individually, the way it felt to pet them, the different foods they liked to eat.

On the way back from the farm one day, Dad stopped the tractor when he saw me sitting in the pasture.

"It's almost time for dinner," he said.

I was trying to remember the goat, so I didn't say anything.

"There's a litter of kittens in the barn. Maybe you can catch one."

I went to the tractor and sat on the wheel well. Dad drove into the barn and cut the engine. "Over there," he said, pointing to a small room in the corner of the barn filled with two-by-fours, engine parts, and rusted paint cans. I opened the door and listened for mewing.

My eyes adjusted to the dark. I lifted pieces of wood off the pile in the middle of the room and leaned them against the wall. Underneath the pile of plywood, I found the mama cat lying on her side, looking sick. Seven kittens sucked at her teats. The mama's eyes had dried mucous in the corners. She didn't react when I reached in and picked up one of the kittens by the scruff of its neck. The kitten was white with a black Y shape on its forehead. I carried it out to Dad, who was greasing the tractor.

"Hawk attack," he said. I held the kitten in my palm. It nestled against my curled fingers and closed its eyes.

"Rabies," I said.

I sat down on an old tire and the kitten fell asleep in my lap. Dad pumped the grease gun until red grease dripped from the bearings, pushing the old black grease out onto the floor of the barn.

ALL THE
SHANE
HINTONS

ALL THE SHANE HINTONS

I ask my wife why she picked me out of all the Shane Hintons she could have had.

I think about them, sometimes. I run searches on the internet, look at their social networking profiles, the records of their arrests, their notices of engagement, the results of their college sports careers. They are a little bit like me, maybe.

My wife is beautiful and could have been with the Shane Hinton from Iowa who is a basketball coach, or the Shane Hinton from New Jersey who sells health insurance. They both make more money than I do and are more handsome. They are better at combing their hair. Their beards grow in thicker and they weigh at least fifteen pounds less than me.

I ask my wife why she picked me and she doesn't answer, but that's okay. There are some things you don't want to know, even though you ask your wife over and over again in a whispered voice while she sleeps. There are some things you can't help asking your wife until she wakes up and pushes you to the other side of the bed.

•

Shane Hinton is a convicted rapist and former boxer. The newspaper articles about him are especially unflattering. I write him a letter, but my wife doesn't want him to know our address.

"He gets out of prison in a few months," she says.

"Montana is a long way from here," I say.

"Not by plane," my wife says.

I have to agree.

•

Shane Hinton is a high school football star who slams his motorcycle into a minivan around the corner from our house. He dies instantly, leaving a blood stain on the pavement that I drive over on my way to work. Someone paints his name and jersey number on a stone wall by the road.

The road is lined with mourners. They park their cars and stand in a circle around his blood stain. One of them yells at me to slow down as I drive by. I yell back that they should get out of the road. It's silly to stand around a blood stain.

I go to the high school and find a trophy of his on display outside the office. Next to it is a picture of him kneeling in the grass with his pads on, holding a football on his knee. An administrator comes out of the office.

"Friend of the family?" the administrator asks.

"Kind of," I say.

"I'm sorry for your loss," he says.

I drive home past the blood stain. Within a week, the rain washes it away.

•

Shane Hinton survives a gas station explosion in Pennsylvania. "I smelled smoke and knew something was wrong, so I got the hell out of there. Right after I crossed the street, she went up. I felt the shockwave in my shins."

I download the article onto my hard drive and label the file "Shane Hinton shockwave."

•

Shane Hinton comes to the house to install our new toilets.

"Are you named after the movie?" I ask.

"Shane is a derivative of John," he says.

"Like John the Baptist?" I ask.

He nods. "That will be one hundred dollars," he says.

•

I compile a list of Shane Hintons in a word processor document and send the same query to them all:

Do you realize that your initials are the same as the first two letters of your first name?

Do people always call you Sean? How do you respond?

Has my wife tried to contact you?

Of course I trust my wife, but sometimes it's good to make sure.

•

Shane Hinton is a charity marathon organizer in Tennessee. I send him the questionnaire and a check for five dollars. I write: "I know it's not much, but this is the best I can do right now. I hope this makes a meaningful difference in the fight to cure cancer."

He writes back: "About six months ago, your wife sent a check for twenty dollars. People always call me Sean. It kind of hurts my feelings."

•

One of the Shane Hintons I send the questionnaire to suggests we organize a festival. We could have a barbecue contest and ride our bicycles together, he says. I send out a mass email and the response is enthusiastic. The basketball coach wants to make sure we have plenty of sports equipment.

"We do if you're willing to bring it," I write.

He writes that gas is so expensive that he might as well fly. We can all tell that he's fishing for someone else to offer to bring the equipment.

No one does.

•

We set the date a couple of months before the rapist is released from prison. We don't necessarily want to exclude him, and several of us believe strongly that people deserve second chances, but it also makes us uncomfortable to think about that guy around our wives and daughters. The health insurance salesman is bringing his grandmother. We agree that we don't want the rapist Shane Hinton around his grandmother.

Probably nothing would happen, we tell each other, but it's best to be on the safe side. A bunch of us really do believe in second chances.

My wife handles the graphic design for the invitations and the signs that we'll hang over the different activity stations. She spends hours looking at fonts and picks ones she thinks will make people laugh.

"Look at this one," she says.

"That's funny," I say.

"You didn't laugh."

"I laughed a little bit," I say. "It was just down in my chest, so you couldn't hear it."

•

I file paperwork with the city and call rental companies to see about bringing tables and chairs, an inflatable castle for people who bring kids, and canopies for people to get out of the sun. The guy at the rental company wants to know what the event is for.

"It's for all the Shane Hintons I could find on the internet who could get the time off work," I say.

"I'm a Shane Hinton," he says.

"You can bring two guests. We didn't invite the rapist, so don't mention it to him."

"I won't," he says.

•

I practice my barbecue recipe every Sunday. The trick is low heat, I tell myself. You have to take your time.

My wife hates barbecue, but finishes everything on her plate. That's why I love her.

She gets the proofs of the invitations back from the printer and she isn't happy with the bleed, so she asks for a discount.

It saves us a lot of money.

•

I get a phone call from a blocked number. No one talks when I answer, but I can hear something in the background that sounds like a laundromat. "Hello," I say, over and over. A dryer buzzes and the call ends. I tell my wife about it, but she's busy making a rubric for the barbecue contest and a schedule for the bicycle ride and three-legged race.

There is still a lot of work to be done, and most of the Shane Hintons who have said they will help us are slow to respond to emails.

•

A week before the event, Shane Hintons start arriving on planes from around the country. "It's so temperate here," a Shane Hinton from Quebec says. He takes his family to a theme park and they all get terrible sunburns.

A Shane Hinton from Kansas City shows up and assumes he's staying with us. He says he's in imports and exports, but I think he's probably a drug dealer. Who imports or exports anything from Kansas City?

I don't want to be rude, so I fold out our futon for him. "The black spot is just dirt from our dog," I say. "If you wake up smelling dog, it's probably just the black spot." The drug dealer Shane Hinton doesn't seem to mind. Packages start coming in the mail addressed to him, and he won't let me watch when he opens them. At night he sits on the back porch and smokes something out of a light bulb.

"He makes me feel itchy," I say to my wife in bed, quietly, because our house is small and sound carries well.

"He'll be gone in a few days," my wife says. I curl up next to her.

"Why do you smell like Kansas City?" I ask. She pretends to be asleep.

•

The day finally arrives and I spend all morning hanging signs around the park. My wife tells people where they can set up their grills.

At the opening ceremony, I try to break a bottle of champagne against the podium. After two or three whacks, I give up and uncork the bottle.

"I'm so glad you're all here," I say into the microphone, holding back tears. "There have been so many times—in line at the post office, driving on the freeway, watching someone load grocery bags into a minivan—that I thought I was the only Shane Hinton in the world. It makes my life a lot more bearable to know there are so many other Shane Hintons out there."

My wife takes the bottle of champagne and lifts it to her lips. A little bit dribbles down her chin as she takes a long pull. "Registration for the three-legged race is at the table by the big oak tree," she says. She heads for the oak tree, where a line of Shane Hintons begins to form.

•

We get carried away telling jokes and stories and decide to start the bicycle ride a little bit late. The park has tall boardwalks that go over the river and the swampland. Birds have flown in from up north and sit with their wings open, waiting to grab fish that swim too close to the surface. The riders stick together in a tight pack. We pedal and lean in formation.

A Shane Hinton from Maine, who is a lighthouse attendant, hits a loose board and goes flying over the handlebars. Two more Shane Hintons run over him and also hit the ground. Most of the rest are able to stop in time, but just barely. The lighthouse attendant probably has a broken clavicle, says a nurse Shane Hinton from South Carolina. We decide that's enough bicycle riding and head back to the picnic area, wiping blood from our scrapes.

•

Back at the picnic area, someone is sitting with my wife at the registration table. They are the only two there. Everyone else went on the bicycle ride.

When we get closer, I recognize him from his mug shot.

He isn't supposed to be out yet, I think. He must know what I'm thinking, because he says, "Good behavior," then winks at my wife. She looks uncomfortable.

None of the Shane Hintons admit to inviting him.

•

The barbecue contest goes okay. We all eat too much and the prize goes to a restaurant-owning Shane Hinton from Oklahoma, which doesn't surprise anyone. The rest of the Shane Hintons seem to be having a good time. Their kids pull at their arms and ask to go play in the inflatable castle. I speak to a couple of the Shane Hintons and we decide it's best if we post someone at the castle to make sure that the rapist doesn't end up there by himself.

We really do believe in second chances, but these are kids we're talking about.

•

The three-legged race has to be canceled because no one wants to be paired with the rapist. "Come on, guys," I say. "He's probably not going to rape anyone here. I bet he's changed a lot."

Someone asks why I don't volunteer, but I don't want to be paired with him either. "Come on, guys, I'm already with the drug dealer. He smells funny. I'm taking one for the team." I look at the drug dealer and say, "No offense. I think it's just the drugs."

"Imports and exports," the drug dealer says.

"Right," I say. "I think it's the imports and exports."

•

Things get heated when the rapist is caught spying on the health insurance salesman's grandmother in the bathroom. "You've crossed the line," the health insurance salesman says. "How could you? That's my grandmother. Now she's never going to be able to use a public bathroom again without thinking of your big, stupid face."

The rapist crosses his arms over his chest and a vein in his forehead pops out. A few of us grab the health insurance salesman before he does something regrettable and walk him and his grandmother out to the parking lot.

"It's been fun meeting you all, but this isn't a safe place for us anymore," he says.

"We're going to miss you at the closing ceremony," I say. "There will be pie."

"We'll get a slice at the airport," the health insurance salesman says.

•

The closing ceremony is quiet and boring. My wife has a bunch of novelty awards, but they all seem inappropriate now: "Most Mustache," "Roughest Jeans," "Loudest High Five." She pushes the box under the podium and doesn't tell anybody who won. No one seems to care anyway.

The sun goes down and the Shane Hintons set off a few half-hearted fireworks before the park ranger tells them to stop. They pack up their picnic baskets and load the trunks of their rental cars and give each other hugs and tell each other to expect Christmas cards. The rapist sits on a bench by the parking lot, watching everyone leave.

I take the box of novelty awards and sit down beside him. "It's not that I think you're a bad person," I say, "but you kind of ruined everything."

He stares straight ahead. "I wasn't supposed to leave the state," he says. "They're going to arrest me when I get back."

"You can have these," I say, handing him the box of novelty awards. "Maybe they'll make you feel better."

He opens the box and starts taking out ribbons, reading each one out loud. "Best Laugh: Shane Hinton. Longest Hug: Shane Hinton. Weirdest Smell: Shane Hinton. These are all for me?"

I nod. He sets the ribbons down in his lap and starts crying. "I don't want to go back to prison," he says.

I touch his shoulder. "Lots of people don't want lots of things," I say.

NEVER TRUST THE WEATHER MAN

NEVER TRUST THE WEATHER MAN

The tractor bounced over a hole, knocking me off the side. It ran over me before stalling with the tire just above my pelvis. The back of my head rested in the dirt and tall weeds brushed my cheeks. I hoped for a thunderstorm, but there were no clouds in the sky.

My organs felt compressed. I breathed from different parts of my chest as my ears adjusted to the silence. After a few minutes I couldn't remember what the engine sounded like. The sun was directly above me.

I pulled my cell phone from my shirt pocket and wiped the dust off the screen. The sweat on my fingers left mud smears as I dialed 911.

"What's your emergency?" a woman answered.

"I ran myself over with the tractor."

"Where are you located?"

"The old Simmons place."

"Can you feel your legs?"

"No."

"We'll send somebody out. Is there anything else I can do for you?"

"I think that's it," I said.

It felt like rain. I dialed my dad.

"Ran over myself with the tractor," I said.

"Can you feel your legs?"

"No."

"That's not good."

"Did you get the parts for the disc?"

"Should be in next week," he said.

The dust started to settle and I heard birds from the tree line. I tilted my head back and saw the neighbor walking toward me. He set a bottle of water on my chest.

"Hot as hell out here," he said.

"Yes, sir," I said, trying to drink. I couldn't sit up enough and poured the water into my nostrils.

"You okay?" he asked.

"Waiting to find out," I said.

"Can you feel your legs?"

"No."

"Might rain later," he said, turning around.

My dad's white truck, followed by the ambulance, made its way through a cloud of loose dirt. The ambulance sank into the ground and dad had to pull it out.

"We got lost," the paramedic said.

"No trouble," I said.

The paramedic slid his hand down my side to the point where it went under the wheel. "Does this hurt?" he asked.

"A little," I said.

"Can you feel your legs?"

"No."

"It's keeping you from bleeding out."

"That's lucky," I said.

"It looks pretty bad," he said.

Pretty soon Mom pulled up on the four-wheeler with a cooler strapped to the back. "Dad called," she said. "How are you?"

"Can't feel my legs," I said.

"I brought food."

Mom spread out an old sheet on the dirt next to me and unpacked a picnic, serving fried chicken and potato salad onto paper plates for me and Dad and the paramedic. Dad and the paramedic stirred up dust with their feet as they talked about the tractor wheel.

I took a bite of chicken and looked up at the sun. The grease slid into my throat but I couldn't swallow. Choking, I spit it onto the ground.

"Might rain," Mom said, chewing.

"It might," I said, even though there were still no clouds in the sky.

FOUR FUNERALS

FOUR FUNERALS

I saw a flame on the water a couple of miles out. The Coast Guard found John the next day, washed up on a small island. They pulled the plane and two more bodies from the bottom of a deep channel.

The burial service was in California. The hearse drove away toward the airport.

Jeff wrapped his car around a pole at a spot where the road curves slightly and can catch you if you've been watching the highway for too long, particularly if you've been taking pills.

He lived for a while in a helicopter on the way to the hospital.

I whistled but Rascal lay still. Blood pooled around his head.

The grass didn't grow back for almost a year.

Vera smiled and laughed, tubes coming out of her arms, holding her stomach in pain.

She stopped breathing around dawn. My father held her hand before they took her away.

Two strange dogs in the barn. One had blood on its collar.

The mosquitoes bit through our clothes as we sat on the runway.

We filled the waiting room.

I never figured out which telephone pole he hit.

We took shots, leaning on the railing over the bay. The food was good and the music wasn't bad and the moon was low and small.

We sat on the porch, talking about sackcloth panties. She rocked in the white chair with the peeling paint, looking out at the field.

He laughed and slurred his words.

We looked out the windows at the saltwater marsh below.

I spent all day digging a grave at the edge of the pasture, where the sunlight fell over the trees early in the morning when he always came home.

I dug for a while and put him inside, but the hole wasn't long enough and his neck bent against the dirt. I dragged him out by his front legs.

The wooden handle of the shovel snapped and I went to the barn to find a new one. The cows circled around him, their heads low. They ran away when I came back.

A woman screamed in the police station. I had to walk around the block to get it out of my head.

The Animal Control agent said she needed to see the wounds. I pulled back the sheet. His face was covered with ants and the veins in his neck stuck to the ground.

She told me that her father left the house whistling a sad song the day her grandmother died.

He juggled knives in the kitchen. His pregnant wife gave him disapproving looks from the couch, but I was on the linoleum floor, looking up, awed by the spinning blades.

We spent Christmas Eve at the strip club, sharing lap dances from two women with fake breasts.

I drank beer and played guitar and he lay next to me, our bodies flattening the waist-high grass.

She sang Cherokee songs. The train's coming, she translated.

A picture of us lying in the yard, his paw around my arm.

A picture of us in the back of the plane.

A picture of us smoking cigarettes, cropped out for the slideshow.

A picture of us smiling, eyes closed.

A service in a small church next to a field of strawberries. A pastor staring at me during the prayer, asking people to come forward.

The ground packed in. The sun behind the trees.

Sweat stains on black suits, fresh dirt, dark, the day so humid.

His mother told me I could have some of his ashes. There would be seven pounds.

I read the passage and followed the ceremony but wasn't sure where to stand. Outside, I hugged my uncle for the first time since I was a child.

His friends swore and cried at the podium and I didn't stay for dinner because the church was too empty and the tables were too long and the dishes were too white.

SELF
CLEANING

SELF CLEANING

The man on TV told me that my teeth weren't white enough. He laid out three simple steps to a brighter smile. I rolled over and tried to fall asleep. Three simple steps. I pushed my face into the cushion and licked my teeth. My breath smelled like old ice cream.

The infomercial played for three more hours while I slept. By the time it went off the air, the sun was coming up. I went to the bathroom and stared at myself in the mirror, stretching my lips back as wide as I could. My teeth were yellow and my gums were swollen. I stretched my lips back even wider. It looked like I was trying to smile.

I didn't get any work done around the house that day. Dirty dishes stayed piled in the sink. The trash can overflowed with watermelon rinds. I ran out of clean laundry and wore a pair of sweatpants and no shirt. I'll stop drinking so much coffee, I told myself, and quit smoking. I'll brush with baking soda. I'll floss after every meal.

I turned the TV on and found the infomercial on another channel. A more successful career, the man said. A happier life.

My credit card was almost maxed out, but I called the number at the bottom of the screen. A woman answered. "We have a promotion running," she said, "if you order one for a friend." I ordered a six-month supply for myself and a trial package for my friend, Pete. Pete smoked three packs a day and drank coffee with every meal. His front teeth were dark brown, and he spent all of his time in the garage. It will be an early Christmas present, I told myself. Pete will love it. He needs to get out of that garage. A brighter smile will give him confidence. We'll look great in pictures together.

I checked the mail every day and put the infomercial on while I slept. The man's voice slipped into my dreams. I woke up refreshed, knowing that soon I would have all of the things I had always wanted: a promotion, a happy dog, a thriving social circle, a new used car with dual airbags. There are times in your life when you realize that the biggest obstacle between you and your dreams is your teeth.

When the package came, it was too big to fit in the mailbox. The postman tried to shove it in, but the box hung out over the street. It was bent and torn. I thought about filing a complaint, but instead I hurried inside to open it up.

I spread the tubes of whitening paste out on the kitchen table. I set the trial package aside and thought about how much Pete was going to appreciate it. He'll break out of his funk, I thought. He'll finally get a job. On the weekends we can go canoeing together.

I used the paste every morning and night for a week and applied it after lunch in the bathroom at work. By the next Saturday, my smile was noticeably brighter. The music from the infomercial was stuck in my head. I hummed it on the way to Pete's house.

Pete's garage door was open. He sat behind a child-sized writing desk, watching me walk up the driveway with the box under my arm. "Pete," I said as I stepped into the garage, "have I got a surprise for you. I know you love your coffee and cigarettes."

"I switched to tea," Pete said.

"I know you love your caffeinated beverages," I said. "But what about those terrible stains on your teeth? They're unsightly and, what's more, they're keeping you from the things that you really want in life. There has to be a better way."

Pete took a sip from his mug.

"Think about it," I said. "Your dream job. The perfect woman. Your first driver's license. They all start with a smile. What if I told you there was a way to have all of these things and still keep your crippling addictions to nicotine and caffeine?"

"What about alcohol?" Pete said.

"Alcohol, too," I said. I put the box on Pete's desk. "Inside that box you'll find one month's supply of a whitening paste guaranteed to improve your smile. Then, after the month is up, if you reorder using my reference number printed on the instruction manual, we both get a free month. It's as easy as that."

Pete took the whitening paste out of the box and turned it over, reading the label. "How does it work?" he asked.

"I'm glad you asked. It's a patented formula that actually strips down the contaminated outer layers so that it can expose the untainted whiteness beneath. Did you know that you have, like, a dozen whole layers of tooth that you're not even using? Let's get those puppies out and make them work for you."

"I'll think about it," he said.

"Listen, Pete. Your teeth are disgusting, and you sit around in this garage all day. It's summer. I'll give you a ride to the Department of Motor Vehicles. Use the paste. Let's get your life back on track."

"Give me a ride to the store," Pete said.

I took Pete to the store to buy cigarettes and beer. When I dropped him off back at his house, he smiled at me. His teeth made me sick. There was no room in my life for someone with that kind of teeth.

I started using the paste more than the instructions indicated. I recorded the audio from the infomercial so I could listen to it in my car and on my headphones at work. One day, my supervisor called me into his office.

"Shane," he said. "What's going on?"

I smiled at him. My teeth felt gritty. "Nothing, boss," I said.

"Your numbers are terrible," he said.

"Numbers aren't everything," I said, smiling wider.

"You're fired," he said.

I packed my things into a small box: pictures of my first wife, a souvenir hand drum from Costa Rica, a coffee mug that said "Now We're Cooking With Gas."

On the way home, I parked next to a bridge over the river that ran through the middle of downtown. I could live here, I thought. There's water to brush my teeth with. I could fish for a living, set up a stand by the side of the road and sell smoked mullet. If I moved every few days, I might not even get in trouble for operating a business without a permit.

Instead, I got back in the car and kept driving until I pulled into my driveway. I put a frozen dinner in the microwave and cued up the DVR to the start of the infomercial. When the food was ready, I sat down in front of the TV with my meal and pulled back the thin plastic cover. I pressed play on the remote and watched the infomercial on repeat all night.

I kept dozing off, but every time the infomercial came to its end the silence woke me up to a blue screen with a phone number and payment information in yellow letters. Just before dawn, I got up and brushed my teeth. One of my canines fell out into the sink.

It was whiter than it looked in the mirror, whiter than the porcelain sink. I picked it up and turned it over in my hand. It felt strange seeing the root that had been buried underneath my gums since I was a kid. I pulled back my lips and smiled into the mirror, poking my tongue into the hole in my gum. It looked like a pink tooth.

In the kitchen, I poured a glass of milk and dropped the tooth in. It rested against the side, whiter than the milk. I remembered hearing that the calcium in milk would preserve the tooth if you wanted to get it reattached.

Surprisingly, my mouth felt better without the tooth. The rest of my teeth were still gritty, but the gap where my canine used to be felt right. I relaxed and turned the TV off, then slept through the day and into the evening.

When I woke up, there were three more teeth on the pillow next to my head, stuck in a puddle of drool. I put them in the glass of milk, even though I didn't want to get them put back in. The new spaces in my mouth felt even better than the first one. I tongued them, trying to feel inside the holes they left in my gums. I could almost reach my jawbone.

I started contemplating a change of careers. I knew sales was out of the question. No one would buy anything from me with all of these missing teeth. They would assume I was going to use my commission on methamphetamines.

I brushed my teeth twice after dark, hoping a couple more would loosen up. I applied the whitening paste and left it on longer than the directions called for. Nothing happened. My teeth were as white as they had ever been. I picked up the phone and dialed Pete.

"I lost my job," I said.

"Come on over."

Pete was drinking a mug of tea at his desk when I pulled up. A lit cigarette smoked in his ashtray.

"Losing my teeth, too," I said, smiling so he could see the gaps in my mouth.

"Doesn't look bad," he said.

"Trying to think of what I can do without teeth."

"Harmonica."

I saw the box of whitening paste on the ground next to his desk, unopened. "You haven't used it?" I asked.

"Not my style," he said.

"I don't think we can be friends anymore," I said.

Pete shrugged. He spit toward the front of his garage. The phlegm hit the white stucco wall and dripped down slowly toward the ground. "Want to go bobbing for apples?" he asked.

I put my index finger in my mouth and pressed on my remaining teeth. They felt solid. No movement at all. "Sure," I said. "That's something people with teeth do."

EXCISION

EXCISION

I found the cyst behind my right ear while fixing my hair before work. The teeth of the comb caught it and my vision went blurry from the pain. I pulled my earlobe down and leaned forward to look at it in the mirror. The pustule was the size of my thumb.

At work I tried to answer the phone but pressing the handset to my ear made my eyes water. I went to the bathroom to dig at the inflamed skin with my pocketknife, and blood ran down my neck and stained the collar of my shirt. I tried to clean it off, but for the rest of the day people asked me about it.

I showed it to Jess when she got home. "You should really go to the doctor," she said.

"If it isn't better in a few days," I said.

I couldn't sleep that night. Every time I rolled onto my right side the pain woke me up. After midnight I got up to look at the cyst in the mirror, pulling apart the slit I'd made with my pocketknife. Underneath the surface of the white bulb I thought I could see something poking up. I grabbed a pair of tweezers and jabbed at the sore but couldn't latch on to anything.

The next morning I called in sick to work and lay on the couch, rolling the cyst between my fingers as it bled all over my hand. I watched soap operas while the blood pooled beneath my head and stuck my hair to the pillow. In the afternoon I called the doctor's office. "You should be seen right away," the receptionist said.

By the time I checked in at the front counter I was sweating and dizzy. When they called me from the waiting room I had trouble standing up. The nurse took my arm and led me to a room with a padded table, telling me to lie on my side. "It's a good thing you came in," she said, eyeing the cyst. "This is serious."

She draped a piece of sterile paper over my head and put a green bucket on the floor beneath me. The paper blocked my view, but I could see her soft outline in the light above me. My breath reflected off of the paper and back into my face, making me feel hot and miserable.

When the doctor walked in, I could only see her feet. "We need to cut this out," she said. "Do you understand?"

"Yes," I said.

I felt a sharp pain as the doctor made an incision behind my ear. Blood and pus ran down the side of my face and dripped into the bucket. It smelled terrible. As she pressed harder, the fluid went in my mouth and I spit it against the sterile paper. "Here it is," she said. I felt a tug and heard jingling metal. The doctor wiggled a pair of pliers in front of my face.

"Lawnmower keys," she said. "Have you been looking for these?"

"I have," I said.

"Well here they are," she said. The nurse took the sheet of paper off and wiped away the blood and pus with a wet towel. My eyes adjusted to the light of the room as the doctor taped a bandage to the side of my head. "Doesn't even need stitches," the doctor said, pulling off her gloves. They gave me the keys in a plastic bag at the front desk when I checked out.

At home, I showed the keys to Jess. "Where were they?" she asked.

"Inside my cyst," I said.

"It's always the last place you look," she said.

I went outside and slid onto the vinyl seat of the lawnmower. The keys had pieces of flesh stuck to them, but the engine started immediately when I turned the ignition. The air was cold, soothing the ache behind my ear.

SYMBIONT

SYMBIONT

Carol felt too much hair between her legs. It was thin and straight and six inches long. She looked down and the hair was white. She didn't have white hair.

She sat up on one elbow, choking on her breath. Emerging from her vagina, an old man looked back at her, his nose and eyes and forehead exposed between her legs. She felt hot and full, closed her eyes, and curled her fingers into the old man's hair. She exhaled and made herself wait to inhale again, remembering that she had a tendency to take in too much oxygen. She crossed her fingers over her chest and felt the breath expand in her lungs. She pressed in on her abdomen to reassure herself that she was not filled with an old man whose eyes and nostrils were protruding from her. Part of her dream, she told herself. Part of her dream.

Carol opened her eyes and the old man's face was still there, his green eyes open, his nostrils flaring. The old man raised his eyebrows. She grabbed a fistful of white hair and pulled. The old man's eyes pressed shut and opened again. She pulled harder, but the old man's head didn't move. She bore down with her abdominal muscles, then pulled harder until thin white hair came out in her fist. The old man's eyes watered.

She stood up and looked at herself in the full-length mirror, keeping her legs spread so the old man's ears wouldn't touch her thighs. The old man's hair hung straight down. Carol started to hyperventilate. The old man looked at his own reflection as though surprised to see himself sticking out of Carol's crotch. Carol made herself wait to inhale. She was dizzy.

"Okay," she said. "What's your name?" She knew the old man couldn't answer because his mouth was inside her. She thought she felt his jaw moving, but no sound came out. They looked at each other in the mirror.

Carol went back to bed and spent the morning typing her symptoms into her laptop. Some websites told her to go see a doctor right away, but there were also forums dedicated to groups of people who believed it was natural for some women, sometimes, to wake up with an old man's head sticking out of them. They called it "the beautiful symbiosis." Carol's breathing slowed. She poked the old man on the nose and got out of bed.

When she sat down on the toilet, the old man's hair hung down into the water. She arched her back and tried to angle the stream of urine away from his face, but it splashed against the underside of his nose and ran into his eyes and hair. The old man sneezed and it tickled her. She wiped his face with a wad of toilet paper. Little pieces of wet paper balled up and collected on his skin. She picked them off his face with her fingernails.

After breakfast, Carol went for a walk. The weather was warm, and she wore a thin skirt that caught the breeze and pressed against the mound of the old man's head. Her gait was short and awkward and her legs got tired quickly. His ears chafed her thighs when she started to sweat. She sat down on a bench, watching traffic pass and stroking the old man's head through her skirt. When she got home she took the skirt off so that the old man could see.

In the afternoon, her father called to talk about his upcoming doctor's appointments, speculating whether the pain in his back was a tumor or just a series of cramps. She put him on speakerphone and the old man rolled his eyes. Carol's father was a hypochondriac.

"I'm pretty sure it's a tumor," he said. "My bones feel too big."

"You always think it's a tumor, Dad."

"You'll be sorry you said that when I'm dead. Most people never think it's a tumor and then—boom—tumor."

"How's Mom?"

"Well, the bad news is I think she's got a tumor, too. In her ankle. She keeps rolling it in the shower. The dog might have a tumor or two, also. There's something wrong with his hearing."

•

The next day was Monday, and Carol picked out a long dress to wear to work. The old man's head wouldn't fit into jeans or slacks. She looked at herself in the mirror before leaving and could only barely see the shape of his head. She lifted the dress and gave the old man a thumbs-up.

At work, she waddled into her cubicle and made her morning calls. Her department had a meeting and, while her coworkers pretended to take notes on their laptops, Carol stared at the table and tried to feel the old man move. She wasn't sure if she could feel his breath in her pubic hair or if it was just the air conditioning.

She sat by herself in the cafe at lunch, but Brad from accounting put his tray down next to hers. Two weeks earlier, Brad had taken her to see a terrible 3-D movie that gave her a headache, and later when they fucked she had bitten her lip to distract herself from the pain.

"You should have come to the party on Saturday," Brad said. "Didn't you get my email?"

Carol smiled. "I wasn't feeling well."

"Is it that stomach thing that's been going around? Jerry had it last week. Said he thought he was going to die. Said his wife made him sign an updated will before she would drive him to the hospital. Come on. Let the guy sign in the car, right?"

Carol ate quickly and excused herself, stopping by the bathroom on the way back to her cubicle. She locked the stall door and lifted her dress and looked down at the old man. The old man looked annoyed. "I know," she whispered. "I shouldn't have gone out with him. I was lonely. He has nice teeth."

On the bus after work, she stood and held the handrail even though there were open seats. The vibration made her need to piss and she tried to squeeze her legs together to hold it in, but the old man's head was in the way. By the time she got to her stop a little bit was dribbling down the bridge of the old man's nose and staining the front of her skirt. She took off her sweater and held it in front of her as she walked home from the bus stop.

She took off her dress as soon as she walked in the front door. The old man's nose was wrinkled in disgust. "I'm sorry," she said. "I had to hold it. The toilets at work are gross." She squatted over the edge of the tub, leaning as far forward as she could, but when she peed it still went in the old man's nose and eyes.

Carol turned on the shower and then got in to wash away the piss. The old man squeezed his eyes shut, and she rubbed shampoo into his long white hair. Carol thought about Brad from accounting and realized she had forgotten to take her birth control pill that morning. There didn't seem to be much point in taking them anymore. Nothing was getting in there.

When she stepped out of the shower to dry off, she rubbed the towel on the old man's head and his thin white hair fluffed up. Carol laughed and the old man moved his eyes back and forth, trying to see what was so funny. She turned so that he could see himself in the mirror, and she could tell by the shape of his eyes that he was smiling.

•

The sound of the old man's breathing woke Carol up in the middle of the night. He was phlegmy. Mucous ran out of his nose and onto her labia. She touched his forehead and could tell he was running a fever. Crust formed in the corners of his eyes and she wiped it onto her thigh.

She couldn't go back to sleep, so she opened her laptop and checked the symbiosis forums for advice. She wondered if she had an unnoticed urinary tract infection and the bacteria had gotten into his brain when she peed.

Women on the forums traded home remedies for when their symbionts got sick. One said she stuck garlic cloves in her symbiont's ears. Another squatted over a pot of steaming water mixed with lemon juice.

In the morning, the old man's fever still hadn't come down, so Carol called in sick to work and went to the walk-in clinic. In the waiting room, she read a magazine that listed sex tips for uninsured women. "Don't let things get too rough," it said.

The doctor told her to change into a paper gown and put her feet in the metal stirrups. "How long have you been symbiotic?" he asked.

"Just a few days," Carol said.

"Standard procedure is to remove the symbiont." The doctor shined a flashlight in the old man's eyes. "He's sick, and he might get you sick."

"I've read they can recover," Carol said.

"That's true, but not always. Is there a history of symbiosis in your family?"

"Not that I know of."

"We can give you a high dose of antibiotics, but we don't really understand how things pass between you and your symbiont. There's no guarantee the medicine will reach him."

Carol stared up at the ceiling where someone had taped political cartoons about the price of gas. "I'll take the antibiotics."

The doctor gave her a prescription and told her to rest, to keep the old man's head elevated, and to call 911 if he became unresponsive.

The pills they gave her were large and hard to swallow. Carol lay in bed with her hips on a pillow and read to the old man. He looked up at the corner of the ceiling. Carol thought he looked like he might have been in the military at some point. "Were you ever a pilot?" she asked. The old man raised his eyebrows. Carol fell asleep with the paperback open on her chest.

In the morning the old man seemed to be doing better. Carol took two more of the large pills and went to the bus stop. At work, she skipped lunch and sat on the patio with the smokers. She noticed one of them giving her a funny look and realized the shape of the old man's head was visible through her dress. She hurried inside.

Brad cornered her in the hallway by the bathroom. "You never emailed me back. Do you have plans Friday?" He looked hopeful, leaning forward on the balls of his feet.

•

Friday evening, she put on her makeup in the bathroom mirror while the old man watched. Brad picked her up at exactly eight o'clock. She was waiting by the front door when he pulled into the driveway. She got in the car and Brad drove with his arm out the window, letting the wind lift his hand. Brad talked about work and Carol couldn't pay attention. She wondered if the old man had a mouth. She wondered what he would say.

Brad took her to a chain restaurant. The waitress gave Carol a sympathetic look when Brad ordered two drinks for himself. "It's happy hour for another thirty minutes," he said. "Buy one, get one free."

"I don't drink," Carol said.

Brad ordered an appetizer that came with five different dipping sauces. Carol tried the first one and it was terrible, so she just sat with her hands crossed in her lap, stroking the old man's head. Brad talked a lot and laughed at his own jokes. Carol looked over his shoulder at the baseball game on TV.

Brad ordered another two drinks and started leaning forward on the table as he talked. Carol leaned back.

"You know what I hate?" Brad said. "Taxes." He laughed. Carol smiled politely.

The waitress boxed up their food when they were done. Brad was unsteady on his feet as they walked out to his car.

"Are you sure you can drive?" Carol asked.

"I'm fine," Brad said, but on the way back to her house he drove too fast and ran a red light. He turned up the stereo and tapped his fingers on the steering wheel. When they got to her house, Brad turned the car off in her driveway. "Aren't you going to invite me in?"

"I don't think so," Carol said.

"Why are you so upset?"

"I just have a sad face," Carol said as she got out of the car.

"I don't even think you tried the dipping sauces."

"See you Monday." Carol shut the car door.

Brad spun his tires as he pulled out of the driveway. Carol stood in the yard, watching his taillights disappear around the corner, caressing the old man's head through the fabric of her skirt.

MIGUELITO

MIGUELITO

When my first wife moved out, she took the pictures of our basset hound and left the pictures of our honeymoon. She took the kitchen appliances we received as wedding presents. She took the bed we bought with our first tax refund.

It was the end of summer. There were papers scattered around the front room. Our health insurance statement, our car insurance statement, and our homeowner's insurance statement were in a loose pile where our desk used to be. I pulled the twin mattress from the guest bedroom into the middle of the living room. The dog sat by the front door, whining.

I slept with the lights on. The ceiling fan spun overhead, casting shadows on the ceiling. I woke up around midnight and let the dog outside. When I woke up again to his scratching at the back door, the sun was coming up.

I rubbed my eyes as he walked in the door, the fur on his paws and long ears wet with dew. He had never stayed outside all night. I figured he must have been waiting for my first wife's car to pull into the driveway. "Sorry, boy," I said. "I don't think she's coming home." The dog shook the dew out of his fur and looked up at me, drool collecting in the corner of his mouth.

I made coffee and went on to the front porch to smoke a cigarette. The mosquitoes were so bad that summer they swarmed throughout the night and into the morning, when you expected them to be sleeping. I exhaled clouds of smoke wherever I saw one circling. My dad told me growing up that mosquitoes didn't like smoke. When we went camping, I always sat in the trail of smoke from the campfire, hoping to keep them away. My cigarette burned down to the filter. The day was already hot.

I took inventory of the things my first wife left behind: one large plate, one small plate, one fork, one knife, one spoon, a whisk, a small filing cabinet, two pillows, a wool blanket, an 8x10 photograph from our wedding. I piled all of these things in the living room next to the twin mattress and thought about how easily they would fit in a box, or a fire pit.

The dog sniffed at the pile of things. He looked confused. "That makes two of us," I said, not knowing what else to say. I sat down on the tile and leaned against the drywall. The dog put his head in my lap. I scratched behind his ears and picked up the wedding photo. Each guest had written their advice around the matte border. I read the tiny inscriptions out loud to the dog.

"Never go to bed angry. Never criticize each other, even in jest. Always say 'I love you' first thing in the morning. Eat a light lunch and a reasonable dinner. Maximize your productivity by making a series of small goals you know you can accomplish. Reinstall your operating system every six to twelve months. Remember how to tie a necktie by repeating to yourself, 'Over, under, around, and through.' Paint the backside of a tick with fingernail polish so that you don't accidentally break off its head."

The air conditioner kicked on. The weather forecast said to expect record highs.

•

I took the dog for a long walk that afternoon. We were both out of shape. We walked through a neighborhood of houses built from only three different blueprints. They were different colors, but you could recognize them by their front porches. One had columns, one had an archway, and one had a railing. I counted them off. "One," I said to my dog as we passed a house with columns. "Two," I said as we passed one with an archway. "Three," I said as we passed one with a railing.

We followed the road until it dead-ended into an open field. A footpath picked up where the pavement ended. We kept walking.

Sweat stung my eyes.

Around a patch of trees, we came to a small pond. A young boy was on the bank, poking something with a stick. I smelled decay as we got closer. The dog sniffed the air.

"What's that?" I asked. The boy stepped back. A small dead alligator was on the ground beside him.

"I didn't do it," he said.

"You have to get a permit to kill alligators," I said.

"I was just poking it."

"Looks like it's been dead a while."

"Is it true they make wallets out of them?"

I nodded. "Shoes, too."

The dog strained at the end of the leash. The baby alligator's skin was split open. Something had been eating its innards.

"What's your name?" I asked.

"Miguel," the boy said.

"Come home with me, Miguel. My house is empty."

"What kind of dog is that?" he asked. "What's his name?"

"What do you think his name should be?" I asked.

"Noodle," Miguel said without hesitating.

"Noodle is a good name," I said, petting the dog on the head. "We're going to call you Noodle." The dog's tongue hung out the side of his mouth. My first wife had named him without asking me. "What do you want for dinner, Miguel? I was thinking about making macaroni and cheese."

"I love macaroni and cheese. My mom makes it for me when my dad has to work late."

"Mine, too," I said.

•

We were both sweaty when we got back to the house. Noodle lay on the white tile, spreading his legs out to let more of his surface area touch the cool floor. Miguel poked through my books. "You read a lot," he said, "but you don't have a lot of furniture. Where do you sit when you read?"

I pointed to a corner of the living room. "Over there," I said. "I just bundle up a blanket and put it behind me."

"That's a funny way to sit," Miguel said.

"I need to take a shower," I said.

"You do kind of smell," he said.

"You, too. There are towels in the guest bathroom if you need one."

"What can I wear?" he asked, pointing to his shirt. It was soaked with sweat and covered in dirt stains.

"I'll pull something out for you," I said. I dug through my clothes, pulling out the smallest ones I could find. I laid out a pair of gym shorts and an old football shirt I wore to do yard work.

"Thanks," Miguel said.

I walked to the bathroom and shut the door behind me.

When I came back out to the living room, Miguel was sitting in the corner with a blanket bunched up behind his back, reading *Don Quixote*. "Have you ever read that?" I asked.

"No," he said.

"Neither have I," I said. "I hear it's good."

"It's okay so far," he said. My clothes were too big for him.

"I'm going to start a wash. I'll throw in your clothes," I said. Miguel didn't look up from his book. After I started the washing machine, I poked my head back into the living room. "I'll have dinner ready in fifteen minutes." Miguel kept reading.

I put the plates of macaroni and cheese on the dining room table and Miguel sat down with me to eat.

"Your house is almost empty," Miguel said, chewing.

"My wife left," I said. "She took most of our stuff."

"Are you sad?"

"A little."

"What about Noodle?"

"I think so."

"Do you love her?"

"I used to, but not anymore."

"Is she pretty?"

"Yes."

Miguel scraped the last of the orange cheese-flavored paste off his plate, then sat down in the corner and started reading again.

"You can sleep out here," I said, pointing to the mattress on the floor. "I'll take the bedroom. Turn out the light when you're done."

I laid a blanket out flat on the carpet in the bedroom and put some dirty clothes under my head for a pillow. My first wife always said she didn't want kids. She wanted to get a PhD. She wanted to work for a non-profit. I wondered what she would think of Miguel, how she would find him socially relevant, what clothes she would want to dress him in. I stared up at the fan, then got up and turned it off. The electricity bill was due.

•

I woke up before Miguel the next morning and went outside to smoke. The mosquitoes landed between the hairs on my arm. I watched one insert its proboscis into my skin. It left behind a blood smear when I slapped it.

Miguel came outside halfway through my cigarette and sat with me on the porch. My gym shorts went down past his knees. "You shouldn't smoke," he said. "My grandmother died from cancer."

"Mine, too," I said. "Will you call my wife?"

"Sure," Miguel said. I dialed the number on my cell phone and hit send before handing it to him. I lit another cigarette. Miguel gave me an annoyed look, but held the phone to his face. "Hello," he said when she picked up the phone. "No, this is Miguelito. I'm here with Shane. He says he's doing fine. We gave your dog a new name. I think he likes it better. We're calling him Noodle."

"Tell her I didn't even notice that she took anything," I said.

"Shane says he doesn't even know what you took. Probably nothing important, he says." The boy's voice sounded as nonchalant as I'd hoped.

"Tell her the dog doesn't miss her."

"Noodle doesn't even miss you. He doesn't sit by the front door whining or anything. Okay. I'll tell him." Miguel hung up the phone.

"What did she say?" I asked.

"She said not to call her any more. She said she's moving to Miami."

I thought about that for a while and lit another cigarette. "Makes sense," I said.

"She sounded pretty. Are you sure you don't want her back?"

"One day you'll understand," I said. "Who wants Pop-Tarts?"

Miguel smiled.

"Pop-Tarts it is."

•

Miguel's school was less than a mile from my house. We walked together on the side of the road, the dew soaking into the fabric of our shoes. The school buses lined up beside us. I drove by the school almost every day but had never been inside. Miguel and I walked up to the front of the building and one of the teachers came over to us.

"Good morning, Miguel," she said. Miguel smiled. "Who's this?" She looked up at me.

"That's Mr. Hinton," Miguel said.

The teacher reached out to shake my hand. "Mr. Hinton, there's a PTA meeting after school. Can we expect to see you there?"

I nodded. "Have a good day, Miguel," I said. The boy looked back over his shoulder at me and smiled as he walked into the building.

•

I showed up early for the PTA meeting. Miguel came down a wide staircase in the middle of the school to meet me. "How was your day?" I asked. "Do you have any homework?"

"Nah," Miguel said. I knew he was lying, but I didn't care. I wanted to take him back to the pond, to see if the baby alligator was still there. I thought maybe we could skin it and make something together. Maybe we could make him a new pair of shoes to wear to school.

The PTA meeting was in the cafeteria. The teacher I'd met that morning held the door open for us. "Good to see you," she said. "There are refreshments at the back of the room."

Miguel grabbed a juice box and a cookie from the refreshment table. I picked up a small bag of chips but put it back down. I had to start watching my weight. We sat in the back row.

The principal took the stage and stood behind a podium. "Let's get the meeting started," she said. "We have a few items on the agenda today. Number one: bugs. We all know it's been a terrible summer for mosquitoes and ticks. Some of us have contracted Lyme disease. One of our best science teachers is out in New Mexico for the rest of the semester being treated. It's hit the science department pretty hard. They can't even bring themselves to properly maintain their equipment." The principal gestured to a group of teachers standing together against a wall. Their heads were lowered in shame. "We're not even sure we can have a science fair if morale stays this low," she said.

The crowd murmured. Miguel pulled on my sleeve and I leaned down so he could whisper to me. "I already started my experiment," he said. "It's about what kind of cheese grows mold the quickest. I had to spend twenty dollars on cheese." The boy looked worried. I raised my hand. The principal pointed at me.

"I know how much the science fair means to these students," I said, gesturing to Miguel. "I'm willing to donate one year's supply of bug spray to the school, to be sent home with every student and faculty member, in order to assure that there are no missed educational opportunities. Let's not forget who the dominant species is here. Are we going to let a few ticks keep our kids from reaching their full potential?"

A teacher in the front row stood up and turned around to look at me. She started clapping. The rest of the room picked it up, and pretty soon the cafeteria was ringing with applause. I waved. The principal closed the meeting. "Don't let anyone say I never solve problems," she said. "Meeting adjourned."

•

Miguel and I walked Noodle back to the pond. The sun was going down and the mosquitoes were especially thick. Miguel slapped one on his neck, and then one on his forehead, and before long he was covered in bloody dots. When we got back to the pond we looked everywhere for the dead alligator, but couldn't find it. "Something must have eaten it," Miguel said. "You're not going to give us the bug spray, are you?"

"Why do you think that?"

"You don't have any money. You can't even afford furniture."

It was true. I hadn't adjusted my budget for a single income. I did the numbers in my head quickly and realized that I'd be coming up short every month. "I guess not," I said.

"It's okay," Miguel said. "I hate that place. Everyone is mean to me."

"What about your cheeses?" I asked.

"Cheese is made from mold," he said, throwing a stick out into the pond. Noodle swam out to get it, and as he swam back to shore a small alligator slid into the water from the opposite bank.

INTERSECTION

INTERSECTION

The car crashed into our living room the afternoon of July third. I was in the kitchen making sandwiches while my wife watched our son play in the back yard. The driver had been drinking.

A busy street dead ends into our house, and for years people have been hitting our exterior walls. Sometimes they swerve and only clip a corner of the house; sometimes they hit the brakes and skid to a stop in the driveway, denting the metal garage door.

This drunk driver never even slowed down until he was parked in our living room. His blue sedan made it all the way down the hallway, tearing out the walls of our son's bedroom and upending our couch on his hood. He stopped just inches short of the kitchen bar.

I put my half-made sandwich down on the plate and went to the driver's side window. The driver looked stunned. His windshield was covered in drywall dust. "Are you okay?" I asked.

"Nice couch," he said, rubbing his jaw. The airbag left bright red marks on his cheeks. I wondered if he had head trauma.

When the police showed up, they told me that this kind of thing was expected around the holidays. They said I could press charges for reckless endangerment, but in the spirit of the season that maybe I should just let it go. My wife held our son in the wreckage of our living room. "I guess we can let it slide this time," I said. They took the driver away in handcuffs to let him sleep it off in jail and left his blue sedan in the middle of our living room.

"We'll send over a tow truck," the officer told me. "Happy fourth."

The insurance company refused to pay anything for the damages. I sat on hold for three hours that afternoon, staring down the hallway toward the garage. It was strange to see sunlight on the tile floor.

"I'm sorry this is taking so long," the woman from the insurance company said. "Most people are off for the holiday."

"It's okay," I said.

After a couple more hours, she told me there was nothing they could do. "Call back on Monday," she said. "My manager is out on a camping trip for the long weekend."

My wife wasn't happy. "What do we pay them for?" she asked.

"It's considered an act of God," I told her. "They have special exemptions for this kind of thing."

Our son was scared. "Are there more cars coming?"

"No," I said, looking down the hallway as a bright red pickup truck squealed to a stop at the intersection.

"Where can I sleep?" he asked.

"In our room. We're going to have a slumber party," I said. The master bedroom was on the opposite side of the house. It was the only room still intact.

It rained that night as we cuddled in our bed. The wind blew up the open hallway. Every time there was a strong gust, our son sat straight up. "I think I heard a car," he said. I grabbed the flashlight from my bedside table and shined it down the hallway toward the living room. It reflected off the chrome grille of the blue sedan.

"Just the wind," I said. "No more cars."

"How will the other cars know to stop?" he asked.

"There are signs," I said. "And reflectors. Tomorrow we can paint something on the wall."

In the morning, we pulled our chairs around the hood of the blue sedan, since our dining room table was in splinters. The yolks of our eggs slid toward the front of the car. It was Sunday morning, and normally my wife would be excited to see the new week of coupons in the newspaper, but she just stared down at her reflection in the blue paint. "When are they going to take this car away?" she asked.

I shrugged. Our son ate a bite of his eggs and pushed the plate away. "Can I play video games?" he asked. We all looked at where our flat screen lay face down on the tile floor.

"We'll get a new TV," I said. "Maybe you can read your book."

My wife cleared our plates. The egg yolks had dried on the low side, congealing into crescent-moon shapes.

I went to the hardware store and stood in line at the customer service desk. "My house has a large hole in it," I said. "The outside is coming inside."

"You're going to be wanting plywood," the man behind the desk said, pointing to a corner of the store. "Aisle twenty-three."

In the plywood section, I got the attention of another employee who was trying to hurry past me. "The man at the customer service desk says I need plywood, but I don't know what kind. I was thinking maybe maple?"

"That's not how it works," the employee said, looking over my shoulder. "What are you using it for?"

"A hole in my house," I said. "A house hole."

"All right. Plywood is measured by thickness. For the kind of hole you're describing, I'm imagining you'll want something in the three-quarter to one-inch range. How big is this hole?"

"Roughly car-sized," I said.

"And you're mainly looking to keep out the elements, I'd imagine? Also, pests? Crickets, roaches, pygmy rattlesnakes?"

"Exactly," I said, even though I'd never heard of pygmy rattlesnakes.

The employee smiled. "I think I have a handle on the situation. I'd like to set you up with three sheets of three-quarter-inch plywood. It won't last forever, but it should make it through the summer, unless it's an especially active tropical weather season."

"They're saying it might be," I said.

"That's outside of my expertise. What I can tell you is that this plywood will last through as many as three hurricanes or five tropical storms, depending, of course, on the severity, distance from the eye, and location of first landfall. That much I can tell you."

I bought the plywood and the employee helped me strap it to the top of my car. He tied a red plastic flag to the end to warn other drivers that the plywood was sticking out beyond the edges of my car. "Is this legal?" I asked.

"Not strictly, but we do it all the time," the employee said. He patted the top of my car and leaned into the window as I started the ignition. "Have a good day."

At home, my son stood by the foot of the ladder as I screwed the plywood into the stucco. When I was done, I pulled out a can of green spray paint.

"We can write something here for the cars to see," I said. "What do you want it to say?"

"Happy birthday, America. Don't drive drunk," my son said.

I spray-painted the words in all capital letters across the plywood.

"It looks very festive," I said. My son was happy with himself. He stood with his hands on his hips, and I could see a little bit of the man he would become.

For lunch, I started the grill and we sat on the back porch. Smoke from our neighbors' grills rose over the privacy fences and oak trees. When I looked out, away from the sliding glass doors, I could almost imagine that there wasn't a blue sedan parked in our living room.

I cooked a package of hot dogs and put them on buns. "That's too many hot dogs," my wife said.

"I thought we might see who could eat the most," I said. "Like they do every year on TV. They dip them in glasses of water first so the bread goes down their throats easier."

"I just want one," she said.

"Can I have pickles on mine?" our son asked.

"Relish is the traditional condiment," I said, "but I guess it's okay."

That evening we watched fireworks on the TV in our bedroom, the red and green and yellow flashes changing the colors of the walls. Our son smiled at the shapes they made in the sky, but every time one exploded with an especially loud boom, he looked down the hallway to where we had covered the hole with plywood. The sheets hadn't lined up perfectly, and in the dark I could see the glow from the street lights and the shadows of passing cars.

We slept a little better that night. The plywood muffled the sound of traffic and kept the mosquitoes out. My son woke me up once, talking in his sleep. I thought he said something about drywall repair, but that was impossible. He knew even less than I did about home maintenance.

When the holiday weekend was over, I went back to work and tried to forget about the car in our living room. By lunchtime I had become increasingly anxious. The sound of the fax machine made me jump. On my lunch break, I called the insurance company. "Can you come get the car out of our living room?" I asked the woman.

"We're still processing your claim," she said. "As you can imagine, the holiday season is a busy time for us."

"Any idea how long it might take? My wife really wants it out of there."

"I'd guess seven to ten business days, assuming we can find a tow company that doesn't have a waiting list."

"I understand," I said.

"Thank you for your patience."

For the rest of the day, I tried not to drink any caffeine. I kept imagining my wife and son sitting on the couch as an eighteen wheeler plowed into the living room. I imagined them splattered on the metal grille. I imagined the driver sitting outside my house with his head in his hands, giving a statement to the police. Would they know how to reach me? I checked my cell phone. No missed calls.

On the way home I got stuck in traffic. I tried to call my wife, but her phone went straight to voicemail. She's okay, I told myself. She always forgets to plug her phone in, and the battery doesn't last as long as it used to. She probably took our son to the park. They're probably talking about what a nice day it is. He's probably sweating through the thick white sunscreen she makes him use.

The traffic stretched ahead of me for miles. I turned on the radio but couldn't concentrate on what they were saying. "Government spending is out of control. What we need are fewer traffic lights and more prisons. This country was built on Coca-Cola and hand grenades, not seat belts and dental floss."

Traffic stayed stop-and-go all the way to our neighborhood. A fireman directed cars past our house. I parked on the lawn. The sheets of plywood we had nailed over the hole in the wall were splintered.

My wife and son were on the front porch, covered in a thick emergency blanket, drinking bottled water. A police officer stood in front of them with a notepad.

"What's going on here?" I asked as I walked up to them.

"Dad," my son said, running to wrap his arms around me. He cried into the leg of my slacks.

My wife looked away and started sobbing. The police officer pointed at the front door. "Might want to have a look," he said.

I opened the front door. The living room was full of cars. Red, black, green, and white. The metal twisted together. I couldn't tell minivans from pickup trucks from hatchbacks.

"How did this happen?" I asked.

"They were all headed home after the long weekend," the cop said. "You know how it is. One takes a wrong turn and the rest follow. We figure the whole thing was over in less than five minutes."

"Are you okay?" I asked my wife.

"We have to move," she said.

"What about the drivers?" I asked.

"A few died," the cop said. "We're pulling the bodies out now. We should be out of your way by dinner time."

It took the firemen two more hours to remove all of the bodies from the wreckage. They wrenched open doors and trunks with the Jaws of Life. Paramedics loaded corpses onto gurneys, covered them with white sheets, and put them in the backs of ambulances. Our tile floor was bloody. My wife went into the kitchen and boiled spaghetti. She emptied a jar of sauce onto the noodles.

One of the cars had taken down an electrical pole and our power was out, so we ate in the dark.

"Are the dead people ghosts now?" my son asked.

"Not yet," I said. "Finish your dinner."

That night I lay in bed with my wife and son until they fell asleep, then got up and put my clothes back on. The moonlight came in through our sliding glass door and reflected off the wreckage. The street outside was quiet. I could hear my footsteps on the tile.

As I got closer to the wreckage, I heard a low hiss and a faint rattle that I thought might be a cooling engine. I leaned into the spaces where doors and windshields used to be but couldn't see anything. The sound quickened and I could also hear dripping. Finally I got down on my knees. Underneath the pile, a middle-aged woman in a brown dress with yellow flowers looked up at me. Her lower jaw was missing. When she exhaled, blood bubbled from the hole in her neck.

"They missed one," I said to the woman.

She nodded anxiously.

I sat down and leaned against the wreckage, took my phone out of my pocket and dialed the insurance company. I knew the dying woman was a liability. The phone rang three times and went to a recording. I hung up.

"This is going to have to wait until morning," I said to the dying woman. She looked disappointed, but I could see that she understood.

LOW OCTANE

LOW OCTANE

Sunoco tightened her fingers around the handle of the red plastic gas can. The empty can swung against her legs as she walked down the side of the road. It was past midnight and the traffic on the highway made a breeze that ruffled her shirt. The breeze felt good. Her face and arms were sunburned, and the skin was hot and inflamed.

She could make out the sign for the Circle K in the distance, up the unlit highway, but guessed it was still about a mile away. The gas can bounced off her right thigh. Two gallons. A small can. Easy to carry home. Two gallons, a four-mile walk.

There wasn't much to do in the Coochee Valley except hang out at the Shipwreck, a local bar landlocked by at least forty miles. Sunoco didn't like the Shipwreck. It was dark and the draughts were expensive, but a two-gallon can of gas was only running about seven dollars and fifty cents that summer, even at the peak of vacation season, when tourists were pulling off I-75 to fill up on their way to or from the Keys or Miami or Fort Lauderdale in RVs and SUVs and on motorcycles with stereos and cupholders. The Circle K and the Shipwreck were almost side by side, as much as anything in the Valley could be said to be side by side; there was no more than a half mile between them. As Sunoco passed the Shipwreck, the front door opened. A man in a leather jacket stumbled out and fell to his knees in the dirt.

In the parking lot of the Circle K, Sunoco put the red gas can down next to pump number four and waved at the attendant inside the store.

Georgios was on shift that night. She smiled. Pudgy little Georgios with his curly hair and dark skin. Georgios looked out at her and turned on the pump. She lifted the handle for eighty-seven octane and placed the nozzle in the tiny gas tank. She regretted briefly that she couldn't afford the high octane. Her dad would not have approved. He had named her after the highest octane unleaded gasoline available when she was born. He died a couple months after they made Sunoco the official fuel of NASCAR. He had never been prouder. Her dad always said he picked winners. That day, ten years old, she felt like one.

She filled up the tiny gas can and carried it over to the front of the store, setting it down next to the ashtray-trashcan. She smiled at Georgios, but he stared down at his cash register, pretending to hit buttons on the touch screen. The tattoos on her forearms looked discolored in the fluorescent light. Flowers of different shapes and sizes tangled from her wrists upward, lined with thorny stems. Sometimes she suspected the artist had hidden words in the twists of the stems. Her tattoos were bad. The only tattoo shop nearby was next to the interstate in a small building about as wide as two cars. Sunoco got her first tattoo done there when she was fifteen: white and gray feathered angel's wings on her shoulder blades. It had only been a few years, but the ink was already fading.

She went to the self-serve chili, took one of the paper bowls in hand, and lifted the metal lid of the container. She scratched the ladle around the bottom, lifted it, and found it empty. "Georgios," she said, "you're out of chili."

Georgios looked up at her and shuffled from behind the counter. There was no one else in the store. She could feel how nervous she was making him by the way he grabbed a new bag of chili out of the back and dumped it into the container, glancing up at the security camera every few seconds. "It'll take a minute to warm up," Georgios said.

"It's okay," Sunoco said. "I've got time."

Georgios went back behind the register and opened a car magazine. Sunoco leaned against the counter in front of him, trying to see what he was looking at. It was a spread of the new Mustang. Georgios didn't turn the page. His dark cheeks grew red.

"It wouldn't be the Circle K without Georgios," Sunoco said. "I'd like to give you a hug sometime."

"We're not allowed to touch customers," Georgios said, glancing up at the security camera again. "The boss watches the tapes. He'll think I'm stealing candy bars or something. He always thinks I'm stealing."

Sunoco smiled. "You want a candy bar? I've got an extra dollar."

Georgios shook his head. "No eating on shift."

"You like that new Mustang?" Sunoco asked, pointing her chin at the page in front of Georgios.

"It's okay," he said. Georgios' car was out front. It was a small Japanese sedan, about twelve years old, Sunoco guessed. Circle K money wasn't buying him a new Mustang. Sunoco would rather walk than drive a Japanese car.

Even though he drove a piece of shit foreign car, Sunoco liked Georgios. He was quiet, and every time she came in he was reading a different kind of magazine. Sunoco suspected that he didn't have more than a passing interest in most of the subjects: hunting, fishing, teen heartthrobs, Civil War history. "Why does your boss let you read those magazines?" she asked. "Doesn't he make you buy them?"

"I'm careful with them," Georgios said. "I don't crease the pages or take out the subscription cards. He told me one screw up and I could forget about it, but I'm careful. I keep them in perfect condition. He checks."

A buzzer went off by the chili warmer and Georgios pointed at it. "Chili's ready," he said.

Sunoco filled a cup of chili, got a large fountain drink, and grabbed a handful of paper napkins from the dispenser. "I'm a messy eater," she said when she saw Georgios staring at her. "You know me."

"Just don't take too many," Georgios said. "The boss has been giving me a hard time about it." He looked up again at the security camera.

Sunoco paid for the chili and the two gallons of gas and the fountain drink and had enough left over for a single cigar. She picked out one from the case behind Georgios, green apple flavored. Counting the quarters she slid across the counter, Georgios dropped them into the register. He didn't meet her eyes as he said, "Thank you."

Outside, on the curb in front of the store, she ate the chili while looking up at the neon sign by the side of the road. Citgo. Cheap communist shit. Her dad would hate it. She finished the chili and the soda and threw them away, checking inside the window to make sure that Georgios wasn't watching. He leaned on the counter, reading the car magazine. She sat back down on the curb, tilted the red gas can into a wad of the paper napkins, held them to her nose, and took a deep breath. Low octane. She could smell it.

The first time she huffed gas had been at Josh Douglas' house after her senior prom. She had been half-drunk on strawberry-flavored malt liquor, and Josh had taken her out to his parents' garage and showed her a can of gas his dad used in his Porsche. When he poured some of the ninety-three octane onto an old shop rag and held it up to her face, she breathed it in, for him.

She remembered this as she stood up from the curb outside the Circle K. The gas had never been quite as good since. She stuck the paper napkins in her pocket and started walking back to her house, the gas sloshing in the can as she swayed with each step, the fuel soaking through the fabric of her pants and feeling cold against her thigh.

There were no streetlights in the Coochee Valley, at least not on the stretch of Highway 301 that took her back to her trailer in Whispering Oaks. There were only the lights over the gas pumps at the Circle K, and then, as she walked farther away from them, the single light over the smashed jon boat impaled on the sign for the Shipwreck. She slowed down as she neared the bar, looking at the cars in the parking lot, seeing if there were any she recognized. A couple of rednecks leaned against the bed of a pickup truck, smoking cigarettes and staring at her. The brims of their baseball caps threw shadows over their faces. Sunoco couldn't tell if she knew them.

"What you got there?" one of the rednecks asked her.

Sunoco looked down at the gas can, still feeling lightheaded, her vision a little blurry but coming back into focus. The red from the gas can reflected red light onto her forearm, changing the colors of the tattooed flowers.

"Gas, I reckon," said the other redneck. They smiled at each other. "Now let's see. Eighty-nine octane?"

The other redneck laughed. "She's eighty-seven if I've ever seen it." He turned his head and spit into the loose dirt in the parking lot. "You need a ride? We're getting out of here."

Sunoco tried to speak but couldn't. She touched the front pocket of her pants and felt the wet napkins there. The rednecks' cigarettes burned close to the filters. They flicked ashes at the ground, sending sparks chasing after them. The light above the parking lot looked green and Sunoco felt the gas wearing off. She got into the cab of the pickup truck and the rednecks got in on either side of her. A wool seat cover scratched against her thighs and an itch started at the backs of her knees and began working its way up toward her hips. She shifted uncomfortably on the bench seat.

"How about leaving that gas can in the back?" the driver asked. "I don't want it splashing on my seats." Sunoco shook her head. The driver shrugged. "Don't think that'll stop me smoking," he said, pulling a fresh cigarette out of his pack. Sunoco reached into the pocket of her pants and pulled out the wad of napkins and held them to her face. When she inhaled, the vapor felt cool against the back of her throat. The movement of the pickup truck backing out of the parking spot and pulling onto the highway rolled her head from side to side.

"Shit, she's huffing it," the other redneck said. He reached over and lifted Sunoco's head by the chin. "Where you headed? We ain't driving all over the Valley tonight."

"Whispering Oaks." Sunoco's own voice sounded foreign to her. It was too deep and slow. Her forearm itched. She put the gas can down between her feet and scratched the spot with her other hand. She could feel the outline of a tattooed rose under her fingertips. Her back itched, and her neck. She moved against the seat back, trying to create friction.

"Bill, she's bleeding," the passenger said. The driver turned on the dome light and leaned over Sunoco. The passenger pressed against the door to get away from her. The spot she had been scratching dripped blood down the side of her arm.

"Come on, sweetheart, don't get that shit on my seat," the driver said. Sunoco held the arm up in front of her face. She wanted to apologize, but couldn't find the words. The blood ran down toward the crook of her elbow, but her forearm kept itching. She kept digging her fingernail into it until she carved out a small hole in the skin. There was something just under the surface. She could feel the lump of it, different than the raised lines of her tattoo.

The truck came to a stop and the passenger jumped out. The driver pushed Sunoco's shoulder. "Out," he said. "Get the fuck out."

She stumbled out of the pickup truck, landing on her stomach in the tall weeds on the side of the road. "Jesus Christ," the passenger said. He threw the gas can out and slammed the door as the driver sped off. The red can landed in the dirt, fuel pouring out of the black spout.

Sunoco spread her fingers into the sand, breathed through her open mouth, and tried to lift her head. Her neck felt weak. Eventually she was able to lift herself onto her elbows. She raised her head above the weeds and looked around, out at the empty field in front of her, at the long, dark highway, at the reflectors in the middle of the road, almost at her eye level, shining back at her as a car passed on the highway.

She scratched at her forearm, dug her fingernails deeper into the skin, feeling something in the dark that she couldn't identify. She pushed her thumb and forefinger into the wound and grabbed something thin and pulled until the pressure in her arm released and the itch subsided. She smiled and reached for the gasoline-soaked napkins. When the next car passed on the highway, she saw the rose sticking out of her skin, its stem wet with her blood, its petals misshapen and bent.

The itch moved to her back and she twisted around in the dirt to scratch it. The rose wobbled as she moved, and she could feel a strange pressure where it had sprouted. It was like feeling a part of herself that she never knew existed. She reached over her shoulders and scratched and scratched until she felt something breaking through the skin of her back, and even in the dark she knew it was a pair of wings. She felt the feathers against her skin.

Sunoco sat up and put the napkin to her face and inhaled. Cars passed on the highway without stopping, and she watched her new shadow on the ground beside her. The wings made her look taller. She put the napkin to her face again and inhaled. The skin around her nose and mouth was cold from the evaporating fuel.

There were other tattoos, on her thighs and ribs and ankles, and they itched, too. She looked at the rose protruding from her forearm and thought about them: the revolver on her upper thigh, the cards on her ribcage, the swallows in the center of her chest, the stars on her ankle. She touched the revolver, then the swallows, then put her fingers to her ankle, where a swirl of stars composed a small galaxy that stretched down to the top of her foot in purples and oranges, traced the outline of them in the dark and began to scratch, fingernails digging as starlight glowed beneath her thinning skin, glistened in her blood, and now poured from her bones and spread out over the asphalt, glinting off oil slicks and cigarette butts, peeling the shadows off tree trunks and fence posts and the sides of passing cars.

NOBODY
LOVES
MR.
IGLESIAS

NOBODY LOVES MR. IGLESIAS

"**S**eventy-five percent of America's trash gets exported right here, out of Tampa Bay," the cop said to me, his leather shoe on my neck, pushing my face down into a paper bag full of liquefied fried chicken. "It's what we call a booming local industry, which is why I've been sent here—when there are people all over town getting shot and robbed and raped, and having serious traffic accidents, and trying to leave their abusive spouses—in order to pull you out of a fucking trash heap. And now my shoes are covered in this shit." He kicked a rotten piece of fruit with his other foot. "And I'm going to have to smell it all fucking day. Can you see why I might be a little bit pissed off, just this very minute?"

"Yes, sir," I tried to say, but his foot was choking me.

"I can't hear you, son." He lifted his foot a little bit.

"Yes, sir, I understand," I said.

Martin and Louis were the guys who worked at the dump, and I thought we had a pretty good relationship. They always told me to stay out of the trash, that it was a liability issue, and that they were going to call the cops on me, but I never thought they actually would. The dump was in a corner of the county that wasn't highly populated, so a lot of the time they would trade off shifts taking naps in the early afternoon. When it was Martin's turn to keep watch for the supervisor or people bringing in trailer loads, I knew that if I waited long enough he'd fall asleep, too, and I could crawl out from the hedges, climb the chain link fence, and hide in the pile of trash before he woke up. I thought we had an understanding.

When you love trash, there are a lot of people who don't trust you. I saw Martin and Louis as brothers of a sort. I knew they weren't as passionate as I was, but they enjoyed their jobs, the proximity to the mounds of stuff, the fillings of lives and deaths and marriages and dissolutions of marriages. You could see it in the way they refused to wear the county-issued masks. You could see it in the way they leaned forward on their toes to look in the backs of pickup trucks.

The cop took me to jail, and I spent the night on one side of a booking cell while the rest of the inmates refused to sit next to me on the bench. "You fucking stink," a car thief named Sean told me.

I didn't call my wife to bail me out. She had been watching my relationship with trash develop over the last couple of years. I think she felt threatened. I tried to tell her trash could never change the way I feel about our family, that it was a supplemental relationship, that the things I found would bring us closer together, but I could sense she didn't believe me. She had stopped telling me when she was going to bed. One minute we'd be sitting on the couch, then I would look up and she'd be gone, asleep in bed without me.

When they released me from jail the following morning, I couldn't get the shoelaces to go back in my shoes. I had to walk away from the jail with my shoes flopping against my feet. It was an indignity, but when you love trash you get used to that kind of thing.

I kept walking, past my neighborhood, until I got to the front gate of the dump. It was close to noon by the time I got there. I knew Martin and Louis would be taking their lunch break soon. I looked down at my arm, but I didn't have a watch on. I sneaked around the side of the fence and huddled in the bushes, watching Martin and Louis relax in their plastic folding chairs. Maybe they had already eaten, I thought. They looked sleepy.

Here's the thing about trash: it grows. You can be arrested one day, taken to the county jail, and the next day, as soon as you get back, it's a whole new ballgame, trash-wise. It never stops coming. Martin and Louis can take short naps, but the pickup trucks roll through the gates, the weight in their beds making the vehicles lean backwards. Old people and young people park on the raised platforms and shovel stuff out onto the pile.

After a short time, Martin and Louis were both asleep, and I climbed over the fence and went down into the trash pile. Mostly, I was looking for love letters. They were hard to find, and usually when you did they were surrounded by signs that the people in them had recently died: medals, prescription bottles, eyeglasses. I liked that stuff, too, but it was the love letters that kept me coming back.

You can ask people to see their love letters, and people just won't let you see them. They think you're kind of creepy for asking. But you can learn a lot about people from their love letters. There's no spellcheck, for one. So people who have learned words by hearing them spoken have a funny way of writing. Once, I found a sticky note that said someone was placed on a "petal stool." If you ask me, that sounds a lot better than a pedestal. If I had to choose something to be placed on, I would choose the petal stool.

I didn't usually find love letters. I usually just found decaying pieces of meat, but I had a feeling about the pile that day. Sometimes the pile calls out to you. It says, "Look over here," or, "Don't step here—there's a lot of nails." That day, the pile was calling to me.

I picked through some bags of kitchen detritus and turned over some cardboard boxes from TVs and refrigerators and window-mounted air conditioners. Love letters aren't usually in those things, but you never know. What you really want to look out for are cigar boxes. Love letters fit especially well inside cigar boxes.

That's why I was so happy when I found the cigar box. When you love trash, and you find a piece of trash that's really good, it's probably the best feeling you can have as a trash lover. It's like when someone who loves music hears a really good song. That's what I think it's probably like.

The cigar box was old and full of letters. I took one out and unfolded it. Down at the bottom of the page it said, "I love you," and there was a lipstick kiss-print. I closed the cigar box carefully, making sure I didn't drop any letters, then headed toward the front gate. Martin and Louis were still asleep. I walked slowly past them, trying not to wake them with the sound of my shoes flopping against the ground.

The letters were addressed to a Mr. Iglesias. He lived just down the street from me in Strawberry Hill, a retirement community nestled against a strawberry farm. There are a lot of strawberry farms around here, and people name neighborhoods after them and then sue the farmers for exposure to pesticides.

I stopped on the sidewalk as I passed my house. The lights were on inside. I wondered what my wife was making for dinner. Maybe I could find Mr. Iglesias and be back before she and my son sat down to eat. I hadn't spoken to them in days.

•

Central Florida is full of retirees. They come here for the sun, because who wants to die in the middle of a blizzard? The snow muffles sound, so nobody can even hear your last words. Down here, everyone can hear you scream. Also, we have a vibrant shuffleboard community.

I walked up to the Strawberry Hill guardhouse and looked past the gate into the rows and rows of manufactured homes, where old people drove slowly on golf carts or sat in small yards, tanning on lawn chairs. The guard slid open the window and looked out at me.

"What do you want?" he asked.

"I'm here to see Mr. Iglesias," I said.

"You're not on the list. And, anyway, Mr. Iglesias isn't taking visitors."

"I have something of his." I held up the cigar box.

"Where did you get that?"

"I found it at the dump."

"You're lucky," the guard said. "His family is here right now. I shouldn't do this, but you have ten minutes." He pushed a button inside the guardhouse and the gate lifted.

"Thank you," I said.

"Ten minutes," he said.

I found the manufactured home with the address from the letters quickly. It was near the pool and shuffleboard court. There was a sedan and a hearse in the driveway outside Mr. Iglesias' trailer. I knocked on the flimsy door.

A woman about my age answered. "What do you want?" she asked.

I held up the cigar box. "I have something for Mr. Iglesias," I said.

"I threw that away last week. Where did you get it?"

"The dump. Are you his daughter?"

"Granddaughter."

"I want to ask him about these love letters."

"Nobody loves my grandfather. He came down here to die, but it's taken him ten years. Those letters are from a Russian prostitute who was hoping that he would marry her for citizenship."

"Don't you think Mr. Iglesias might want to look over them before he goes? He kept them for a reason."

"He's dying right now. Don't you hear his death rattle?"

I listened closely. I thought I had been hearing a window-mounted air conditioner, but I realized it was the sound of an old man dying. I looked back at the hearse. The engine was running and the man in the driver's seat, dressed all in black, tapped his fingers on the steering wheel. "Okay," I said. "I'm sorry to bother you."

Instead of walking back to the guardhouse, I headed for the shuffleboard court. The cigar box was heavy in my hands. I dropped it in a garbage can full of protein shakes and disposable colostomy bags and wondered if I'd see it again some day. A shuffleboard tournament was already in progress. I watched for a few minutes. A banner above the court read "Strawberry Hill Annual Shuffleboard and Family Picnic Day." Families sat together on the benches at the ends of the courts, cheering for their parents and grandparents as they slid the black pucks from one end to the other. A young boy tugged at his grandfather's pants leg between throws. The grandfather bent down and tousled the boy's hair and talked to him until it was his turn again. "Did you see grandpa pull off that shot?" the man asked. "Watch this next one."

Over the music and laughter, I heard the short burst of a siren. The cop who had arrested me at the dump stepped out of his cruiser.

"You again?" he said. "You just don't learn, do you?"

I lifted my hands above my head to show him that I didn't have a weapon. When you love trash, sometimes you have to sacrifice your pride for safety. Some things aren't worth dying for.

DRIVING
SCHOOL

DRIVING SCHOOL

The mechanic had a glass eye and it was hard to tell where he was looking as he walked around my car, checking boxes on a form. He was overweight and exhaled loudly as he knelt down.

"There's your problem," the mechanic said from underneath my front bumper. I got down on my knees and looked where he was pointing. The mangled corpse of a young boy was stuck in the undercarriage, his bones poking through his skin and dripping blood onto the smooth concrete floor of the garage.

"That must have been why that woman came running after me," I said.

The mechanic stood up and wiped his hands on a rag from his back pocket, then walked to the rear of the car. "That her?" he asked, pointing to the body of a woman wedged into the wheel well.

I knelt down to get a better look at her face. "Yeah, that's her," I said. "That must have been why the family at the park started screaming."

"Makes sense," the mechanic said. He pointed at the rear bumper. I bent over again. The family from the park was there, stuck under the rear bumper. They had paper plates and napkins in their hands and stuck to their faces. The child was wearing a pointed birthday hat.

"Let's talk numbers," I said.

The mechanic looked over his notes. "You're looking at extensive structural damage, not to mention funeral arrangements, reparations to next-of-kin, and memorial scholarship funds."

"Think you can take care of it?"

"Give me time to work up an estimate. You can wait in the front room. We have coffee."

I sat down next to a stack of tires and a teenage girl brought me a questionnaire and a cup of black coffee. "Do you have any tea?" I asked the girl, but she was wearing headphones. The coffee was burnt.

The questionnaire tried to gauge my customer loyalty. I answered "Very Likely" when I actually felt "Not Likely At All." When I handed it back to the teenage girl, she gave me another cup of coffee. My bladder was already swelling from the first cup.

After half an hour, the mechanic came back in. "Mr. Hinton," he said, beckoning me to where he stood by the front desk. "It's pretty bad. The bones did a number on your drivetrain, and the memorial scholarship funds have to account for the rising cost of tuition. You're going to get some points on your license, and the press is probably going to get involved. They love this kind of story. Don't be surprised if they make you out to be the bad guy. You have the face for it."

"Can you put me on a payment plan?" I asked.

"I'll give you a twenty percent discount if you take our Road Safety course."

"Sign me up," I said.

The mechanic opened a door behind the front desk. "Back this way," he said.

I followed him through the door into a dark room with five rows of empty chairs. The mechanic handed me a glossy booklet and sat down behind a desk at the front of the room. He leaned back in his chair and propped his feet up. "My name is Wayne," he said, "and I'll be your instructor today. You're here because of a grievous lapse in judgment. My role is not to judge. I want to help you get better. Through this program, with some audio-visual aids and multiple choice worksheets, you will come to understand the importance of taking responsibility for your mistakes. Let's watch a short video about the legal ramifications of leaving the scene of an accident. Turn to page twenty-three in your workbook."

I took a seat in the middle of the room. Staring intently at the computer screen in front of him, Wayne moved the mouse and a projector came to life. On the desktop, he double-clicked a video file titled "Intro." An accident scene appeared on-screen with a woman's voice narrating. A red sedan was twisted and mangled against a light pole. A young man in a black sweatshirt stood next to another car on the side of the road. The camera cut to a closeup of his eyes shifting from side to side.

"So, you're guilty of manslaughter," the woman's voice said. "What happens next? In this informational video, I will walk you through the grieving process and give you some helpful tips for dealing with the press."

The shifty-looking young man jumped into his car and sped away. The camera panned left and the woman came into frame. "If you leave the scene of an accident, you're going to look very guilty," she said. "Take this young man. None of us know what actually happened before this video started, but I think we can all safely assume he's at fault. I can almost guarantee that the police will see it that way. Maybe he was actually very guilty. Maybe, in a fit of road rage, he ran this other car off the road and into a telephone pole, in the process killing the entire family inside. I'm no lawyer, but it sure looks that way to me. How about you? Record your personal response on page twenty-four of your workbook." The video ended.

"Why aren't you writing?" Wayne asked. He raised his eyebrows. I couldn't tell if his glass eye was pointed at me or at the computer screen on his desk. I turned to page twenty-four and started scribbling. "This material will be covered on the test," Wayne said. He didn't give me time to finish writing. "Let's start the next video."

Wayne opened a file and the woman started talking about how to speak to the press. "Answer their questions with questions," she said. "Never admit guilt in front of a camera. Always ask if your responses are on the record."

Wayne leaned back in his chair. I tried to take notes but the room was so dark I could barely see the page. The workbook was thick and heavy. Wayne sneezed and wiped his hand on his pants and I couldn't remember which of his eyes was glass, but I could tell that he was in love with the woman in the video even though he knew they could never be together.

FUMES

FUMES

The dog showed up in the front yard the same day the azaleas bloomed. It was thin, mangy, and covered in sores on its belly and legs from chewing at fleas. I tried to smell the azaleas, but the dog lay in the shade of the bushes, growling at me each time I got close. Azaleas only bloom for a few days each year. I didn't want to miss my chance.

I baited the dog away with bowls of water and dog food, but it wouldn't move. I pulled a steak out of the freezer and waved it at the dog, but the animal just rested its head on its paws. I knew the flowers would smell fantastic. The petals were pink and white.

In the yard, I opened a folding chair and sat down. "You can't stay there forever," I said. The dog looked at me, exhaled deeply, and looked away. It licked its lips. The sun rose above the trees and then started back down. The dog napped, woke up, stretched, and fell back asleep. Sweat soaked through my pants and stuck my legs to the vinyl seat. My feet itched. The sun burned my forehead.

I stuck my nose in the air, and the heat and breeze from the traffic carried the faint scent of the azaleas to me. It was tantalizing. The dog seemed to know what I was thinking. He rose to his feet and the hair on the back of his neck stood up. I looked around for a stick.

To my right was a dead oak limb. I looked at the limb and then back at the dog, trying to figure whether I could reach the limb before the dog reached me. The dog bared its teeth. I leapt for the limb. The dog pounced, and we fell together into the dirt.

I grabbed the dog's throat with my left hand and tried to push it away from my face while my right hand reached for the oak limb. The dog's breath was rank and hot, and its eyes squeezed almost shut as it struggled to bite me. The last thing I remembered was a cramp in my forearm working its way up to the tips of my fingers.

When I woke up in the hospital, I had no idea how much time had passed. My wife and son sat next to the bed, and I tried to speak, but no words came out. The skin on my throat felt tight. Reaching up to it, I felt stitches. My son looked up from his video game.

"Dad!" he said.

My wife smiled. "You're awake," she said.

I held my arms out to them, as if to say, "Come hug me," even though I couldn't speak. They crowded around the bed and rested their heads on my chest. I first noticed the tube coming out of my abdomen when my son's arm bumped it.

"Oh, that," my wife said.

I raised my eyebrows.

"I'll get someone," she said, and gave me a long kiss on the lips before pressing the call button to summon the nurse.

The nurse stuck his head in the door. "You're awake," he said, smiling. "We saw your heartbeat jump on the monitor. Did your wife tell you about the tube?"

My wife looked down at the floor and shook her head. My son pressed his nose against my ribs.

I looked down at the tube. It ran out of my right side and into a machine that pumped rhythmically up and down, then back out of the machine and down to the floor where it disappeared underneath a curtain in the middle of the room.

"Well, you're very lucky," the nurse said, stepping into the room. "We almost lost you, but it turns out this guy," the nurse pulled back the curtain, "was a perfect match."

On the other side of the curtain, the dog lay in a hospital bed with the sheets pulled up to his chin. A brown leather muzzle was over his mouth. My tube ran up under the sheets and into his left side.

My wife started to sob.

"I'll send you home with an informational pamphlet," the nurse said. "It's really an amazing procedure."

They kept me two more days for observation. On the third day, the nurse came in with my discharge paperwork. He pushed a large wheelchair into the room. It had two seats, side by side. He put my arm over his shoulder and helped me up. When I moved, the tube stretched against my side and I grimaced from the pressure. Once I was seated, the nurse pulled back the curtain. "All right," he said to the dog. "It's time for you to go home." He lifted the dog out of the bed. The dog pawed at the air and twisted its head from side to side. "Settle down," he said, and the dog seemed to hear, because it went limp in his arms.

He put the dog in the empty seat next to me. The dog tried to snap at me, but its mouth was still covered by the muzzle. The nurse strapped it to the back of the seat. "He's a little rambunctious," the nurse said, laughing. "What do you think you're going to do with that muzzle on? Stupid dog."

My wife pulled the car around and met us at the front of the hospital. The nurse helped me and the dog into the back seat, then put the machine between us. He buckled the dog's seat belt and the dog tried to bite him. He laughed again. "Stupid dog."

My son got to sit in front. On the way home, he and my wife counted fire hydrants. They counted twenty-three. I stared out the window. The dog squirmed.

For the next month, I stayed in bed. My wife made a pallet on the floor of our bedroom for the dog. She brought my meals to me on a tray. Every time she came in, the dog growled at her through its muzzle. "None for you," she said to the dog. "You eat through a tube now." The dog looked like it wanted to get up, but it was too weak.

I tried to read the pamphlet the doctor sent home with me, but I couldn't even make it through the first fold. My abdomen felt swollen. I still couldn't speak.

My wife started working overtime to pay the medical bills. My son had to walk home from school now, our house key on a string around his neck. When his mother came home after dark, he was tired and grouchy and hadn't done his homework. She cooked dinner and helped him with math problems while I lay in bed, listening to their voices from down the hallway. She couldn't keep up with the chores, with the dog hair that collected in the corners of our bedroom. Even though she never complained, I saw her looking sadly at the vacuum.

After school, my son wanted to play catch. He brought his ball and glove to my bedroom. "Can you get out of bed yet?" he asked.

I started to cry and shook my head. I still couldn't speak. He needed to do his homework, but I couldn't figure out how to tell him. He hung his head, walked away, and I heard his video game start up in the living room.

By the time I recovered from the surgery, I hadn't been outside in a month. In the back of the local weekly I saw an ad for the botanical gardens and pointed at it happily. My wife was exhausted, but the next Sunday she helped me and the dog into the wheelchair, placed the machine on my lap, and took us to the gardens. In the front seat, my son punched his baseball glove as we drove.

The azalea blossoms had died and fallen on the ground, but the roses were in bloom. I gestured to them and my wife pushed the wheelchair in so I could smell. The dog was agitated. I patted him on the head and smiled. He twisted in the seat, working his jaws against the muzzle. The leather stretched but held firm.

My son ran up and down the rows of plants, enjoying the sunshine. A man in a pair of overalls handed us a flier. "Flower smelling contest starts at 2:15," he said. The flier announced a one hundred dollar prize.

We registered and waited by a white gazebo for the contest to start. The registration fee was five dollars, which left my wife with only two dollars in her wallet. She gave it to our son and told him to get a snow cone. "I overdrafted the checking account this morning," she said after the boy ran off.

As people showed up for the contest, the dog grew more restless. My wife fastened the leather straps around his chest so he wouldn't wiggle out of the wheelchair. People in the crowd pointed and whispered, but my wife pretended not to notice.

We were first in line for the contest, and the announcer helped my wife wheel me up on stage. The dog squirmed. I smiled at the audience.

"Ladies and gentlemen," the announcer said, "welcome to the fifty-third annual Tampa Bay Chamber of Commerce Flower Smelling Competition. My name is Harold Merriweather, and aside from my awesome God, my beautiful family, and the best country in the world, I love smelling flowers more than anything. Let's see what this year's contestants are made of."

The announcer wrapped a blindfold around my head and asked if I could see. I put my hands up in front of my face and shook my head. He held the first flower under my nose and I inhaled deeply. I knew the smell at once: honeysuckle. I smiled and opened my mouth, but no sound came out. I stretched my jaw and my tongue and tried to make any sound at all, but nothing happened. The announcer pulled the flower away.

"Well," he said, "do you have a guess?"

I knew it was honeysuckle, but I just shook my head.

"Honeysuckle," the man said.

The announcer went through the rest of the flowers: rose, gardenia, lily. I couldn't say a word. "Thanks for trying," he said, removing the blindfold. The crowd clapped sympathetically. I touched my throat, where my stitches were still held in place with black thread, but the announcer didn't notice. He waved a young woman in a yellow summer dress up onto the stage, blindfolded her, and held a flower under her nose.

"Rose," the young woman said.

"That's right," the announcer said. He put the second flower under her nose.

"Gardenia," the young woman said.

"Right again," the announcer said.

"Honeysuckle," the young woman said. "Lily," the young woman said.

The announcer gave her a check for one hundred dollars. "What are you going to use it for?" he asked.

The young woman smiled and leaned forward so that her mouth was right next to the microphone. "Dental surgery," she said. The crowd cheered.

My wife pushed the wheelchair off the stage and out toward the parking lot. She loaded me and the dog into the back seat. Our son was overheated and fell asleep as soon as the air conditioner turned on. The dog panted, its tongue hanging out between the brown leather straps of its muzzle. Over my wife's shoulder, I could see the gas gauge resting just above empty.

BELL
CREEK

BELL CREEK

Grady had a different cancer every time I saw him. His stomach, he said: weeks to live. His pancreas: six months. His liver: no more booze.

I found him by the creek one evening, drunk and lying in the dirt. "Who the hell are you?" he asked me as I drove up.

"It's me, Grady," I said. "You're not supposed to be here. I locked the gate."

He laughed.

"How's the cancer?" I asked.

"In my bones," he said.

Frogs called from the creek. Grady sat up. "Give me a ride home."

He didn't wait for an answer, just climbed in the bed of the pickup truck. I opened the window. We drove through empty strawberry fields, plowed up for the summer, the dirt loose and gray. "You see my fucking cows?" Grady asked, pointing across a barbed-wire fence. The cows were thin. He had complained for years that the pesticides from the farm were poisoning them.

"Lost any lately?" I asked.

"A calf this week," he said. "Withered to nothing."

I pulled onto the hard road and then into Grady's yard, where his family gathered around a fire pit in front of the house to shoot Roman candles over the cow pasture. The cows huddled in the far corner, pressing against the barbed wire.

"You remember Shane?" Grady asked his wife.

She nodded. "Stay for dinner. You tell him about the cows?"

Kids with dirt-covered faces ran circles beneath the fireworks.

"Can't stay long," I said.

Grady's daughter, Ava, herded her kids away from the fire and sat next to me on a folding chair. "Mr. Shane," she said. "Been a while since we seen you." She was a few years younger than me. We had never talked.

"Ava," Grady said, "get us some beers."

She took two cans of beer from a scarred plastic cooler and leaned over to hand me one, her faded t-shirt hanging low, giving me a view of her bra through the neckline. Grady's grandkids shot more Roman candles out over the pasture. A white dog howled at the glowing orbs.

"It's a hell of a life," Grady said, opening the beer.

•

The next day I saw Ava in a thin brown dress leaning against a fencepost at the edge of Grady's pasture. Sweat stained her armpits.

I drove the tractor in wide ovals in the loose dirt. When I got across the field to where she stood I turned off the tractor and climbed down. A cloud of dust followed me and choked us both. "Nasty out here," I said.

"I brought you a glass of water," she said, holding up a mason jar. Tiny white flakes floated inside. I drank it down in one pull.

"How are the cows?" I asked.

"Sick," she said.

"Pesticides?"

"That, or the heat, or the dust."

Down the fence line, where the creek ran from our property onto Grady's, the cows gathered at the bottom of the embankment, underneath the only trees in the pasture. Their heads were at ground level.

"I heard you got married," Ava said.

"Didn't last."

"Mine either. Any kids?"

"None that I know of," I said. She smiled.

I gave her the jar and she turned around, walking across the pasture to Grady's house. Putting the tractor in gear, I watched her dress move as she walked, climbing up her thighs and falling to her knees.

There were more Roman candles over the trees that night. The cows cried and the white dog howled. I walked over to the fence and watched, smoking, listening to the kids laugh and scream.

Ava got up from a folding chair and came over to where I stood. We leaned against the fence without speaking for a while. The fireworks whined in the air as they burned out.

"They don't make good milk after the kids scare them like this," she said, looking up at the fireworks.

"They're your kids, right?"

"Some of them. The creek's cloudy. You been spraying?"

"Just for weeds."

"The rain must have washed it in there. Let me show you," she said.

I pulled apart the barbed wire and climbed through. Above us, the sky glowed and filled with smoke, the lights from the fireworks making our shadows flicker. She grabbed my hand and pulled me forward.

It was dark by the creek. Trees blocked the light from the fireworks. Ava took off her shoes and waded in. The water came up to her shins.

"You think that's a good idea?" I asked.

"Good enough," she said, splashing around in the water. Even in the dark I could tell it wasn't the right color.

I took off my shoes and joined her. Our feet sunk into the creek bed as I held her waist. I felt her breath on my chest. The water stung my shins.

"The water burns," she said, pulling her dress up over her head. Her skin looked too pale and thin in the moonlight. Her bones were on display. She held my hand and led me farther into the water. The reflection of the moon shattered as we were sucked into the wet sand. I ran my fingers along her ribs.

"The cows drink it?" I asked.

She nodded, pulling my hips into hers, then pushed me down onto my back in the shallow water. She pressed her hands to my chest and straddled me. We made small waves that lapped at the bank.

After we finished, we stepped out of the creek. I dried my hands on my shirt. The chemical stink of weed killer burned my nose. "I'm not sure that water is safe," I said.

"I go in there all the time," she said, pulling her hair into a ponytail.

She kissed me on the cheek. "Go on back through the pasture. I don't want them to see you."

•

In the morning, I walked our side of the fence to the creek. The water was milky. I sat on the bank, looking across the fence for prints. Only our footprints high up on the bank survived in the wet sand.

When I went to the barn to get the tractor Ava was already there, sitting on the seat. Her eyes were puffy and her upper lip was split open.

"What happened?" I asked.

She looked at her hands in her lap. "They think I'm at the store," she said.

"You can stay here."

"You know I can't," she said, climbing off the tractor.

"I'll kill him."

"The poison will kill us first." She smiled sadly.

"I thought you said it was safe."

"I never said it was safe," she said.

I drove the tractor all day, thinking of Ava every time I poured water onto my head to cool off. I looked for her on the fence line, but she never came out of the house.

There were no fireworks over the pasture that night. The lights in the house were on, but I couldn't hear anything from inside. I waited by the creek, expecting Grady or one of his sons or grandsons to show up with a shotgun. The palmettos on the far bank looked like a good place to hide, or the cattails across the fence line. It was the middle of summer, and there were water moccasins and rattlesnakes all through the woods. I wished I had worn boots.

Ava showed up in the same thin brown dress. We sat together on the bank.

"I have these feelings," she said.

"My pants are getting wet," I said.

She kissed me. The scab on her lip felt bigger than it looked.

"What happened to the fireworks?" I asked.

"Too dry," she said, leaving me on the bank with my pants and shoes soaking up the poison water.

I followed her through the pasture and stood at the fence line and watched her go inside. I could see the blue light from the TV on the white curtains. I tried to guess what they were watching.

•

The next day I ran over hog skeletons and tree branches with the tractor, splitting them into tiny pieces. I poured water over my head and my wet skin gathered dust as I drove. That night I smoked, leaning on the fencepost. The barbed wire caught my pants and shirtsleeves and tore small holes in the fabric.

I climbed through the fence and sat by the creek, but kept my shoes on and stayed out of the water. My feet and shins were covered in a heavy rash. To the west, I saw heat lightning in the clouds. It smelled like rain.

I heard a cow walking toward me, and soon it appeared through the palmettos. Her footsteps were heavy and slow. She climbed down the bank and nuzzled me. In the moonlight her white fur looked transparent. I let her lick my hand, leaving a trail of snot and spit as she drew away. She drank from the creek.

As I walked back along the fence it started to drizzle, and soon the rain filled up the low spots in the yard with cut grass and piles of fire ants that floated on top of other piles of fire ants. I stood in the rain and my shins itched. As I scratched the inflamed skin, it broke open. I pulled up my pants and let the rain wash the pus away.

When the rain died down Grady's family came outside and lit a fire in the front yard. I went back down to the creek. The cow was up to her neck in wet sand, her eyes wide. I sat and rubbed her head but she twisted away from me, sucking deeper into the mud.

Grady didn't look up as I walked across his yard. He sat on a folding chair with his feet on the edge of the fire pit. The wood in the fire was wet and sizzled as it burned. The flames were low. Grady's grandkids shot fireworks out over the pasture.

"Bad news," I said. "You got a cow up to her neck in quicksand down there." I pointed out across the field.

Grady stared down into the mouth of his beer can. "Let's go have a look," he said, clenching his jaw.

We stood on the bank and looked down. "Can't hardly keep them out of the mud this year," he said. "I'll get the tractor." I waited next to the creek while Grady went to the barn. The cow moaned and I leaned against a tree.

Grady came back with a small blue tractor and backed it up to the bank. He tossed me a thick cord and I tied it around the cow while Grady hooked it to the tractor. I stood back as he revved the engine and put it into gear.

The cow cried in pain as the motor strained and the tractor inched forward. Grady let off the gas and put it in a lower gear. I heard something snap. Fireworks flew over our heads and into the palmettos on the other side of the creek. The cow screamed. Grady cut the engine.

I knelt down by the animal. Her body bent away from her legs at the wrong angles and her head hung down in the water. She opened her mouth, blowing bubbles that floated toward the fence.

"Guess we have to put this one down," Grady said. I turned around as he stepped off the tractor and picked up a rifle from beside the seat.

Walking back through the trees, I watched Ava from the shadows. She sat by the fire as kids ran circles around her, screaming and lighting fireworks and chasing the white dog. The crack of the rifle blended in with the sound of the fireworks as they lit up the pasture. I heard the tractor start back up and Grady appeared at the top of the steep bank, his face obscured by trails of smoke that drifted just above the ground. I lit a cigarette and sat down, picking the scab from where the poisoned water had blistered my skin.

RELAPSE

RELAPSE

My wife came out of the bathroom with the bloody little air sac in her hand. "There's nothing inside," she said.

"Do you feel better?" I asked. I poked the air sac with my finger.

She nodded. "What should we do? It seems wrong to flush it."

I took the shovel with the splintering handle and dug in the corner of the yard, beneath the branches of an old water oak that had been slowly dying from hurricane damage. I had no idea how deep to bury something so small.

We had already started to talk about names. I repeated them in my head as I dug. *Colette. Clarice. Tristessa.* I piled the dirt next to the hole. *Charles. Douglas. Elton.* The streetlights came on. Squirrels chattered in the tree above me.

I placed the air sac, wrapped in toilet paper, into the hole and covered it with dirt. Bandit, our hound dog, sat next to me. He sniffed the fresh dirt after I packed it in with the shovel.

Neither of us slept much that night. Every time I woke up, my wife was already staring at the ceiling. I put my hand on her stomach, but she didn't look at me. "Do you feel okay?" I asked. Her eyes were open, but she didn't answer. I heard squirrels scratching at the gutters, trying to dig their way into the attic.

In the morning, she got dressed for work like any other day. "You should take the day off," I said. "You need to rest."

She put on her makeup. "I'll call if I need anything," she said.

I opened my first beer at ten o'clock and drank it on the back porch with Bandit. I opened another beer and counted the dead limbs on the old water oak hanging over the neighbor's yard. Seven. Seven dead limbs.

A squirrel ventured down into the yard and Bandit chased it to the fence. I fell asleep in the lawn chair and didn't wake up until my wife's car pulled into the driveway. My face was sunburned. I licked my lips. They were cracked and peeling. I followed my wife inside and took a beer out of the refrigerator.

"You look bad," she said.

"Yard work," I said. We turned and looked out at the yard, overgrown with hitchhiker weeds, untrimmed hedges reaching up past the windows.

"That your first?" she said, pointing at the beer.

"Yes," I said

"I need to lie down," she said.

Bandit scratched at the sliding glass door. When I slid it open, he set a bloody squirrel down at my feet. The squirrel was almost dead. It wheezed as it tried to breathe. Bandit pawed at it and looked up at me. The squirrel's mouth opened and closed. I put the blade of the shovel against the base of its neck and put my weight onto it quickly, severing the rodent's head in one slice, and then buried it in the corner of the yard.

My wife made me an appointment with a therapist for the following day. "No drinking before you go," she told me as she left for work. I sat on the couch and stared at the TV without turning it on. In the middle of the morning, Bandit brought another squirrel carcass to the sliding glass door. I buried it next to the other one.

I put on a nice shirt and brushed my teeth. My hair wouldn't comb down. She probably sees a lot worse, I told myself. I just need a little help. I'm not as bad as most people. My head just hurts. My eyes just look puffy.

On the way to the therapist's office I got nauseated with one of those hangovers that gets worse as the day goes on. I parked the car and went around the side of the building. There was a chain link fence at the top of a bank leading down to a small creek. I pressed my fingers through the chain link and put my head between my legs and threw up yellow bile onto the grass and dead leaves. Across the creek, a feral cat saw me and took off running up the opposite bank.

There was a white noise machine in the waiting room and classical guitar music. I could hear someone crying behind the closed door and tried to read the paperback I brought with me, but I couldn't focus on the plot.

After a few minutes, the door opened and a sniffling woman made her way to the exit. The therapist came in to the waiting room. "Mr. Hinton?" she said. I followed her into the office, and we sat facing each other on chairs with too-large pillows.

"Your hands are shaking," she said.

"I was almost a dad this week," I said.

"Dads are just regular people who are good at pest control."

"I can't do anything about the squirrels in our yard."

"Do they interfere with your sleep?"

"I don't think anyone really sleeps."

"Would you consider medication?"

"I want to get better," I said.

"Make a chart of your emotions," she said, handing me a worksheet. "Put a happy face in this column when you feel good and want to drink. Put a neutral face when you want to drink out of boredom. Put a sad face when you want to drink to forget."

"I forget lots of things," I said.

"Then this should be easy for you," she said.

On the drive home, I held the steering wheel tight to stop my hands from shaking. Bandit was waiting for me at the back door with a pile of squirrel carcasses. I opened a beer and put a sad face on the sheet of paper, then dug four holes in the corner of the yard. I chopped and pulled out twisted piles of roots and placed the dead squirrels in the holes. Bandit stood next to me, wagging his tail.

It rained that night and my wife and I sat on the couch. We ate sushi and opened a bottle of wine. I put a happy face on the sheet of paper. We let Bandit come inside to get out of the storm.

"How was the therapist?" my wife asked. "Did you tell her about the squirrels?"

"She wants me to take medication," I said.

The wind picked up and the power went out.

"I bought poison for the squirrels," my wife said.

"What if the dog gets sick from chewing on them?" I asked.

We saw the outline of the water oak every time lightning lit the sky.

"You'll have to bury them deeper," my wife said.

We heard a series of cracks, then a loud thump, and with the next lightning bolt, we saw the tree laying in the yard, its roots sticking up six feet in the air.

The power was out all night and the house got muggy without the air conditioner. Bandit whined in the living room. Outside the sliding glass door, squirrels ran back and forth in a panic. Bandit scratched at the door, barked, sat down, looked at me. "Not tonight," I said, and shut the blinds.

In the morning, I went outside to survey the damage. The tree had shattered into several large pieces. Squirrels perched on the fallen branches. A swarm of bees swirled around a section of the trunk. Through the split wood, I could see the white of a large hive.

My wife stepped out the door with a cup of coffee in her hand. Bandit chased a squirrel over a branch to the fence. "They'll need a new place to live," my wife said.

My hands shook. "A few more feet and it would have hit the nursery," I said. We had started painting the walls with pictures of circus animals. They were crude and half-finished.

Bandit dove to catch a squirrel and slung it from side to side, snapping its neck. My wife went back inside to get ready for work. I picked up the shovel and started for the corner of the yard.

ABOUT THE AUTHOR

Photo by Keir Magoulas

Shane Hinton holds an MFA from the University of Tampa. He lives in the winter strawberry capital of the world.

ACKNOWLEDGMENTS

Ryan Rivas, who is the best kind of friend a writer can have: a really good editor. Erica Dawson, who is so far in my corner that she's throwing punches on my behalf. Asha Dore, whose superpower is generating writing feedback at an inhuman speed. Lidia Yuknavitch, who told me to keep going when good sense told me clearly to stop. Jeff Parker, who is incredibly generous with both his time and bar tab. Brock Clarke, whom I want to be when I grow up. Mikhail Iossel, who has a better understanding of literature than I would ever be comfortable with, personally. Kevin Moffett, who dresses so well that I'm not totally convinced he's real.